SUCKER'S PORTFOLIO

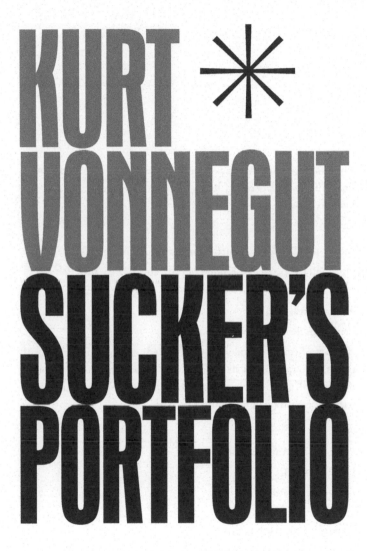

KURT *
VONNEGUT
SUCKER'S
PORTFOLIO

amazonpublishing

Text copyright © 2012 Kurt Vonnegut, Jr. Copyright Trust
Originally released as a Kindle Serial, November 2012.

Published by Amazon Publishing
P.O. Box 400818
Las Vegas, NV 89140

ISBN-13: 9781611099584
ISBN-10: 1611099587
Library of Congress Control Number: 2012922576

EPISODE ONE
BETWEEN TIMID AND TIMBUKTU

I.

A young painter, whose wife had been killed in an automobile accident two weeks before, stood in front of the open French doors of his studio in a silent house. His feet were far apart, as though he were poised to strike someone, and the look of frustration on his face contradicted the peaceful scene before him. A green slope, speckled with bright leaves fallen from the maples, dropped away to a pond that brimmed over the rock dam he had built in the Spring. A stooped, bright-eyed old man, a neighboring farmer, paced slowly up and down the length of a wooden pier that jutted into the pond, casting a red-and-white bass lure into the water again and again and again.

The painter, David Harnden, held a small dictionary in his hands, and, in the frail warmth of Indian Summer's sunlight, he read and reread the definition of the word between *timid* and *Timbuktu*: "the general idea, relation, or fact of continuous or successive existence."

Impatiently, David snapped the book shut between his long fingers. The word was *time*. He ached to understand time, to defy it, to defeat it—to go back, not forward—to go back to the moments with his wife Jeanette, to the moments time had swept away.

The old farmer's fishing reel sang. David looked up to see the bright lure smack the water, sink, and begin its twitching course back to the pier. Now it was dripping in air, inches from the casting rod's tip. The last of the ripples it had made dissipated at the pond's edge. Another instant flickering past—going, going, gone. *Time.*

David's eyes widened. He knew his fascination with time was near lunacy, a flailing about, a reaction to tragedy. Yet, in calmer moments, there was growing a steady conviction that his wish to travel back to happier days might be reasonable. A scientist friend had once remarked audaciously, with a few fingers of whisky in him, that any technical advance that was conceivable to the mind would one day be made a reality by scientists. It was conceivable that man could travel to other planets; that would come to pass. It was conceivable that a machine could be made more intelligent than men; that would come to pass. It was conceivable to David that he might return to Jeanette. He closed his eyes. It was inconceivable that he could never see her again…

He watched as the farmer whipped his rod to make another cast. The pier quivered. "Keep away from the end," called David. He had been meaning to fix two of the uprights, which were green, splitting. The old man gave no sign that he heard. David was in no frame of mind to worry about it. To hell with it—the pier would hold. His thoughts turned inward again.

He stretched out his long frame on a couch in the studio, let the dictionary drop to the floor, and lost himself in a fantasy of visitors from another world. He daydreamed of beings infinitely wiser than men, with more senses than mankind's five; beings who could tell him about time. He thought of visitors from space bringing an understanding of time because it seemed beyond the limits of human minds—far beyond. Perhaps there were in the universe forms of life—the flying-saucer men, say—who scampered through time wherever their fancy took them. They would laugh at earth men, to whom time was a one-way street with a dead end in sight.

Where would he travel in time if he could? David sat up and ran his hands through his short, black hair. "Back to Jeanette," he said aloud—back to the sights and sounds and smells and feel of a May afternoon. Time had fogged, flattened, cooled the precious image. He could remember that the afternoon had been vital, happy, perfect. He could no longer see it clearly...

Vaguely, heartbreakingly so, he could see himself and the handsome, laughing Jeanette as they had been on that day. The perfect moment? There were an infinite number of them, identically lovely. Married two weeks, they had come home to this house on that day... had jubilantly explored every room, exclaimed over the green, rolling tranquility framed in each window... had perched on the rock dam, had swirled bare feet in the rising crest of the pool and kissed...had lain on the slope's new grass...Jeanette, Jeanette, Jeanette...

The image was shattered by a cry. "Help! Help me!"

David jumped to his feet. The two uprights at the pier's end were split, splayed wide. The outermost section of planks hung crazily between them like a sprung gallows trap. The old farmer was gone. Nothing troubled the surface.

David ran down the slope, stripping off clothing as he went, and dived into the stinging chill of the water. In the depths beneath the broken pier, the strength went out of his strokes. Before him loomed the farmer, doubled into a tight ball, motionless save for a gentle lolling in the current. David burst the surface, filled his lungs, and plunged downward again. He seized the shoulder strap of the old man's overalls and tugged at the passive mass. No struggle, no clawing, no death grip.

David worked over the body on the slope. He lost track of how long he had been working to wring death out of the farmer's lungs. Up, over, press, relax...up, over, press, relax... How long had it been since he had shouted to a small boy on the road to get a doctor? *Up, over...* No flicker of life in the gaping white face. David's arms and shoulders ached; he could no longer close his hands into fists. Time had won again—had stolen another human being from those who loved him. Suddenly, David was aware that he had been talking aloud the whole time, angrily—that he was behaving, not with the grave concern of a man saving a life, but with the rage of a brawler. He felt no emotion toward the man under his hands, felt only hate for their common tormentor—time.

Tires swished through the deep gravel of the driveway above. A short, overweight little man trotted down the slope, swinging a black bag wildly as he came. David nodded wearily. Middle-aged Dr. Boyle, the village's only doctor, nodded back, struggling to regain his breath.

"Signs of life?" panted the doctor. He had opened his bag and was now holding a long-needled hypodermic syringe up to the sunlight. He pressed the plunger until a droplet grew at the needle's tip.

"He's dead, Doc—deader than hell," said David. "Thirty minutes ago he was thinking of bass for dinner. Now he's gone. Thirty minutes, all going one way, leaving him behind."

Dr. Boyle looked at him with mild puzzlement, then shrugged. "You'd be surprised how tough it is to kill some of these old turkeys," he said, almost cheerfully. He and David turned the farmer over. Matter-of-factly, Dr. Boyle drove the long needle into the drowned man's heart. "If there's a twitch left in him, we'll get him going again good as new. Maybe." He rolled the body on its stomach again. "You've had your rest. Back to work, my boy."

While Dr. Boyle rubbed the man's limbs and David gave artificial respiration, the barest tint of pink came into the waxen cheeks. A gasp, a sigh, and the old man breathed again.

"Back from the dead," whispered David, awed.

"If you like being melodramatic about it, we're bringing him back from the dead, I suppose," said Dr. Boyle, lighting a cigarette, keeping his eyes on the drowned man's face.

"Did we or didn't we?"

"A matter of defining your terms," said Boyle. It was obvious that the subject bored him. "Drowned men, electrocuted men, suffocated men, they're usually perfectly good men—good lungs, good heart, kidneys, liver, everything in first-rate shape. They're dead is all. If you catch a situation like that quick enough, sometimes you can do something with it." He gave the farmer another injection, this time in the arm. "Yep, back from the dead for a few more years of fishing."

"What's it like to be dead?" said David. "Maybe he can tell us."

"Let's not get corny," said the doctor absently. He frowned. "What's a youngster like you doing brooding about death, anyway? You're good for another sixty years." He colored, laid his hand on David's shoulder. "Sorry—forgot."

"What will he tell us?" insisted David, untroubled by the slip.

The doctor studied him curiously. "What's it like to be dead? In a word: dead. That's what it's like." He put his stethoscope to the old man's now-pounding heart. "What will our friend tell us?" He shook his head. "He'll say what it's customary to say. You've read it a hundred times in newspaper stories. The back-from-the-deaders don't remember a thing, so ninety percent say the customary phrase just to be interesting." He snapped his fingers. "And it's so much bunk. Know the phrase I mean?"

"No. Up to now I haven't been interested."

Dr. Boyle fished a pencil stub and a scrap of paper from his vest pocket. He scrawled a sentence on the paper and handed it to David. "Here. Don't look at it until our protégé comes around enough to talk. Five dollars says we'll hear him say what I've just written."

David folded the paper, kept it in his palm. Together, they carried the farmer up to the house.

II.

David and Dr. Boyle sat on the couch before the living room fireplace. David had built a fire. It was evening, and the two had been drinking. From a bedroom adjacent to the living room came the gentle snores of the old farmer, who now slept away his exhaustion swathed in blankets. There was no room for him in the doctor's ten-bed hospital.

"If you'd taken my bet, I'd be five dollars richer," said Boyle jovially.

David nodded. He still had the slip of paper on which the doctor had written the words he expected the farmer to say. When the farmer had gathered strength enough to speak an hour ago, he had said the words— almost exactly. David reread the slip aloud: "*My whole life passed before my eyes.*"

"What could be more trite?" said Dr. Boyle, refilling his glass.

"How do you know it isn't true?"

Boyle sighed condescendingly. "Does an intelligent man like you really need to have someone else give him the reason?" He raised his eyebrows. "If his life *did* pass before his eyes, his brain was what saw it. That's all anybody's got to see with. If his heart stops pumping, his brain doesn't get any blood. It can't work without blood. His brain couldn't work. Therefore, he couldn't see his life passing before his eyes. QED, quod erat demonstrandum, as they said in Rome and your high-school geometry class—what was to be demonstrated is demonstrated." He stood. "How about my getting some more ice, eh?" He went into the kitchen at the back of the house, the least bit unsteady, humming.

David stood and stretched, and became aware that the heat of the blazing logs, an empty stomach, and the quick succession of highballs had conspired to make him very drunk. He felt buoyant, not wildly happy, but clever. Hazily, he had the impression of being on the verge of outwitting time—of being about to rise above it, about to go wherever he liked into the past.

Now, without quite understanding why, he was in the darkened bedroom, shaking the shoulder of the sleeping farmer. "Wake up!" he said urgently. "Come on, I've got to talk to you." He was rough, irritated that the farmer should continue to sleep. It was somehow awfully impor-tant that he talk to the man immediately. "Wake up, do you hear?"

The farmer stirred, stared up at him with bewildered red eyes.

"What did you see when you were dead?" David demanded.

The farmer licked his lips, blinked. "My whole life—" he began.

"I know that. What I want to know is the details. Did you see people and places you'd forgotten all about?"

The farmer closed his eyes, frowned in concentration. "I'm awful tired. I can't think." He stroked his temples. "It was quick, kind of like a movie going real fast, I guess—kind of flashes of old times."

"Did you get a good look at anything?" urged David tensely.

"Please, can't I go back to sleep?"

"As soon as you answer me. Can you describe anything in detail?"

The farmer licked his lips. "My mother and father— I saw them real good," he said thickly. "They looked young, just a couple of kids, almost. They was just back from the fair at Chicago, bringing me souvenirs, and carrying on about how there was an electric train running clear around the fairgrounds..." His voice trailed off.

"What did they say?" David shook his shoulder again.

"Father said he hadn't spent near as much as he'd expected." The voice was now a whisper. David had to lean over the bed to hear. "Said he had a lot of money left over."

"How much money?"

"Said he had fifty-seven bucks." The farmer was seized by a coughing fit that made him sit up.

"What else did he say?" said David excitedly, when the coughing stopped.

The farmer now looked up with fright in his eyes. "Said he had three bucks more than he needed for a new Therma-King range." He collapsed back on the pillows, his eyes closed.

"Dave! Get out of there!" said Dr. Boyle sharply. His round body was a belligerent silhouette in the bedroom door. "He isn't out of the woods by a long shot. Do you want to kill him?" He gathered up a fistful of David's sleeve and angrily pulled him out of the room.

David didn't resist, hardly knew what was happening to him. He said nothing, left untouched the fresh drink Boyle had mixed for him. He stretched out full length on the couch, with great effort wrote the number fifty-seven under the words on the scrap of paper, and fell asleep—to dream of Jeanette.

III.

"I'm sorry, the doctor doesn't have office hours on Wednesday afternoons," said the white-haired nurse, smoothing her uniform over her bony hips.

"It's a personal call. He's a friend of mine. I have something very important to show him," said David breathlessly. "Where is he—in his study?"

The nurse looked dubious, flicked on an intercommunication set on her desk. "Dr. Boyle, a young man out here says he has something important to show you. Says he's a friend. What was your name, young man?" She watched him alertly, as though she expected him to snatch her gold-capped fountain pen and run.

"David Harnden." David realized from the look she gave him how disreputable he must seem. For a week now, ever since he had saved the farmer from drowning, he hadn't shaved or even washed, except to cool his head occasionally with a cold washcloth. Ineffectually, he tried to straighten his suit, which was twisted in ungainly creases over his body. His trouser cuffs were spattered with clay. He had strode through a rainstorm in the suit on his way to the village library in the morning, lain in it on the wet green slope where he and Jeanette had lain not yet six months ago—

"Dr. Boyle is busy," said the nurse. "Sorry." It was plain that she wasn't.

David leaned over the intercom set, turned on the switch. "Boyle, listen. This time I've got something really big, conclusive. Even you'll be convinced when you see this." He waved a photostat before the microphone.

"Look, Dave"—Dr. Boyle's voice was tired, impatient sounding—"I've got a big meeting on Monday in Albany, and I'm supposed to have a paper ready for it. Thanks to your hounding and a measles epidemic, I haven't gotten beyond paragraph one. Whatever it is you've got, it can wait until after Monday. I can't see you today, and that's that." There was a click in the loudspeaker.

"He can't hear you," said the nurse primly. "He's pulled the plug out." She went over to the door and held it open. "The doctor can see you Tuesday," she said, as though only *she* could hear what Boyle said over the system. "If you'd like to leave that paper—whatever it is—perhaps he could look at it over the weekend."

David was looking up the carpeted staircase, wondering where in the huge old house the study might be. Absently, he handed the photostat to the nurse.

She studied it superciliously. "And what is he supposed to do with this? I doubt if he's in the market for a woodstove. 'Ladies, trade your old range for a Therma-King.' I don't get it."

"It's not for you to get," said David irritably. "Give it back. I'm taking it up to him myself, right now."

She opened the door wider and held the photostat against her spare bosom. "I'll take it up to him. Just tell me what it's all about."

"Tell him this proves the farmer wasn't lying. The Chicago World's Fair was in 1893, and in 1893 you could get a Therma-King range for fifty-four dollars. This ad from an 1893 paper proves it. That's three dollars less than fifty-seven, which is what the farmer said." He turned his back on her. "Oh, to hell with you. You're not listening."

"I can hear you all over the house," complained Dr. Boyle from the head of the stairs.

"Boyle, I've got proof that the old man's life really did pass before his eyes. He traveled back in time to 1893!"

"He should have shot your grandfather while he was back there. Maybe I'd have a minute's peace now to finish this paper."

"Can't I talk to you just a minute?" said David.

"Oh…all right. I'll see you as a patient in critical condition. You're in bad mental shape, Dave. You need to get away and rest like nobody I know, with the exception of myself. Come on up."

"The doctor will see you," said the nurse briskly. She handed him the photostat with patronizing deference.

"I can communicate quite well without the help of an interpreter," said David acidly, and went up the steps two at a time.

Dr. Boyle closed the door to his study, and, with his head resting on folded arms on the desktop, he listened to David's news.

"And this ad clinches it, doesn't it?" David was saying. "The old man went back to when he was seven years old, heard his father talking about the electric railroad at the World's Fair, then give the brand name and price on a kitchen range he was going to buy. It all checks!"

Boyle didn't raise his head. "I don't know what the explanation is, Dave, but I know it isn't yours. The guy has a hell of a memory, maybe. He must. Maybe going under the way he did does something screwy to the mind. Sometimes hypnotists can get people to remember things like the make of car their grade school teacher drove. Something in that line, maybe. Time travel? Hooey."

"I checked his memory, and it's nothing wonderful," said David. "I tell you, I haven't thought about anything else for the past week, and I've been over all the angles. The old man couldn't tell me within ten dollars what the stove he's got now cost him, and he was wrong about the make." He thrust his hands into his pockets. "Give me one solid argument against time travel. There isn't one."

"Logic, my boy," said Dr. Boyle patiently, between his teeth. "It doesn't make sense. You could go back in time, kill a man, and wipe out God-knows-how-many descendants. Knock off Charlemagne, and you kill about every white man on earth. Ridiculous! Why don't you go into gunrunning and sell the ancient Athenians a couple of machine guns so they can win the Peloponnesian War? Why not go back and invent the lightbulb, the telephone, and the airplane before Edison, Bell, and the Wrights get around to it? Think of the royalties!"

David nodded. "I know, I know—those arguments threw me, too, for a while. Then I realized that the old man, if he really did travel through time, didn't go anywhere but where he'd already been. If I say that a dead man is free to travel back to any instant in his own lifetime, then your logic can't lay a finger on it. I don't think he can change a thing about his lifetime, as you very logically point out. If he travels back, he can feel only what he felt then, do what he did then. I'm convinced that that much is possible."

"Who cares?"

"I care," said David evenly. "You care, everybody cares. If it's true, this is a helluva sight more merciful life than it now appears to be."

Dr. Boyle stood, and now he, like the nurse, was holding the door open. "It's a very interesting idea, Dave, a fine one to kick around on a long winter evening. You believe it, and I don't. Neither one of us has a leg to stand on. I haven't got any more time for kicking ideas around, so you're going to have to excuse me."

"You've got to help me find out whether there's anything to it." David backed away from the door, stubbornly settled into an overstuffed chair, and lit a cigarette.

"Look, my friend," said Boyle with exasperation, "a week ago, I hardly knew you. Now I find you dogging me like my Siamese twin. Telephone calls, interminable conversations—all about time, time, time. I'm not interested, do you understand? Why don't you attach yourself to someone who would be? A close friend, maybe a minister or a psychologist, or some kind of ologist who would go big for this sort of monkey business. I'm a general practitioner, and a damned busy one."

"A physician's the only one who can help me with my experiment, and you're the only one in town," said David helplessly. "I'm sorry I'm cluttering up your life. The whole thing seems so important, is all—terribly important. I thought you'd see it that way, too, and want to help. What *could* be more important than proving I'm right? If your afterlife is going to be made up of eternity in the best moments of this life, wouldn't you like to know about it?"

Dr. Boyle yawned. "And if one's life happens to stink through no fault of his own?"

"Then he can settle for a trip back to the womb. Some don't want any more than that."

"You've got it all figured out, haven't you, Dave?" Boyle narrowed his eyes. "How could I help you? What is this experiment you're talking about?" His question had a carefulness about it, the same sort of carefulness he used when probing an abdomen for the knotted muscles of appendicitis.

David handed him another newspaper clipping, this one but a day old. He trembled slightly, keeping his temper in check. This smug little doctor, on whom so much depended, hadn't a grain of curiosity or imagination. He could not see that time—not cancer or heart disease or any other disease in his books—was the most frightening, crippling plague of mankind.

Dr. Boyle was reading the clipping aloud. "Ummmm. 'Los Angeles—A surgeon of the Sacred Heart Hospital here today—' Oh, yes, I read this. The man died on the operating table, and the surgeon revived him by massaging his heart. Uh-huh. Very interesting case, and particularly so to you, I suppose. I wonder if the patient said *his* whole life passed before his eyes?" He put the question sardonically.

"He was unconscious an hour ago," said David.

"How on earth do you know?"

"I telephoned the hospital just before I came here."

Dr. Boyle's eyebrows shot up. "You did *what?* You telephoned all the way to Los Angeles to ask about a complete stranger?" He laid his hand on David's shoulder. "You *are* in bad shape, Dave. I didn't realize what an obsession it was. You've got to leave this idea alone and get some rest—get away from that gloomy house. I'm giving you doctor's orders, now. You're on your way to a first-class crack-up. I mean it. Pack up and get away today."

"I'll get rest after the experiment   plenty of rest," said David evenly. "But the experiment comes first."

"And that experiment is—?"

David saw in Boyle's reddening face that the doctor had guessed. "An operation is what I want from you, Doctor. I'll pay anything you like for it—plenty. I want to see about time for myself." His voice was almost casual. He felt no awe for what he was asking for, felt only a longing for it. "I want you to kill me and bring me back to life."

"Get out," said Dr. Boyle quietly. "Never bother me again, do you understand? Now beat it."

IV.

Two months had passed since Dr. Boyle ordered David out of his office. David leaned back in a deep chair in his studio, propped his feet on his drafting table, and dialed a number.

"Dr. Boyle's office." It was the nurse's voice. She managed by her tone to convey that whoever was calling, whatever his business might be, he was imposing trivia on a vastly important organization.

"I'd like to speak to the doctor," said David. "It's urgent."

"This is Mr. Harnden, if I'm not mistaken."

"You're not mistaken."

"The doctor doesn't want to be bothered by you again. I thought he'd made that quite clear."

"This is an emergency," said David sharply. "If you don't put me through to Dr. Boyle right now, you're going to be one angel of mercy in damn serious trouble."

There was a long silence, unbroken save for her heavy breathing. Finally, a click. "Doctor, it's Mr. Harnden again. I know you gave orders that he wasn't to bother you, but he says it's an emergency." The last word was seasoned with sarcasm.

Boyle sighed. "OK, put him on."

"I'm already on, Boyle. I'm good and sick, or I wouldn't have taken a second of your precious time. You've got to come out here."

"You can't make it to the office? I've got ten patients waiting, and you caught me in the middle of setting a broken arm."

"Sorry, but you're going to have to come out here. Temperature's up to a hundred and two. I'm too groggy to drive." David gave the doctor an imposing list of symptoms.

"Sounds like that two-day virus business that's making the rounds. Can you hold out until four?"

"All right. You'll promise to be here at four sharp?"

"Four it is, Dave," he said tentatively. He cleared his throat. "Are you still worked up about time and all that?"

"No, that's all over now. I was out of my head, I guess, and I'm sorry. I took your advice. It was good advice. Thanks."

"That's good news." Dr. Boyle's voice was hearty now. "I was sorry about the rough treatment I handed you. I should have been more understanding. Look, if you think you could use some psychiatric help, there's a good man over in Troy I could—"

"No, no. I'm all cured. What I need now is some good old-fashioned medicine for a sore throat, a belly-ache, and a fever."

"All right. Hold on until four. A couple aspirin will make you a little more comfortable. If things get worse, give me another ring, and I'll come right on out."

"I'll be waiting," said David. "Walk right in. You'll find me bedded down in the studio." He picked up a hypodermic syringe from the table beside him and turned it this way and that, catching the image of the elm logs' quiet blue flame in the fireplace. "I'll be waiting," he said again, and hung up. He had never felt better in his life.

A coiled spring, sheathed in a metal cylinder, was fixed to the top of the syringe in such a way that it pressed against the plunger. David filled the syringe with water. Two wires led from the cylinder, and he connected these to a battery and a switch. He closed the switch and grunted with satisfaction as an electric trigger released the spring, the plunger eased home, and a fine jet of water shot from the needle. Perfect.

He permitted himself the childish pleasure of feeling mysterious, of imagining what an outsider might make of the scene. It was a winter's high noon, darker than autumn twilight, without snow to brighten the overcast countryside. To the outsider, David reflected cheerfully, Nature would be seeming to sympathize with macabre doings in the studio. Desultory rain from a pocket of warmth thousands of feet above earth spattered and froze on the windowsills.

The parcel had arrived from the instrument maker's only an hour before. He had laid out the special hypodermic syringe and the timelock on the table. They looked like jewelry against their black velvet wrappings. They had only to be wired into the circuit lying on the floor and bolted into place. Everything else had been ready for weeks—the straps nailed to the floor, the bars across the two windows and French doors, the pulmotor—all awaiting the implements that David hadn't had the skill to build.

He didn't need Boyle now. Not at first. He could manage the first part himself. Then the doctor would have to help. Ethically, he couldn't refuse once the experiment was under way.

He laid the syringe and battery and switch on the floor, next to the straps nailed to the naked boards. Now for the timelock. It was mounted on a steel plate, and he twisted thick bolts through the plate into waiting holes in the studio's inner door. David gathered the wires leading from the lock's clockwork and connected these, too, to the switch and battery.

Again he closed the switch. Again the plunger of the syringe was driven down. David cocked his head as, simultaneously, the clockwork began to tick. For one minute, then two, then three, nothing happened save for the ticking. Suddenly, the clockwork whirred busily, and the tongue of the lock was drawn back, freeing the door.

He reset the lock and clockwork, expressionlessly filled the syringe with an oily, colorless fluid, and dialed his phone again.

"Western Union."

"Could you give me the correct time?" said David.

"Twelve twenty-nine and a quarter, sir."

"Thank you." David set his watch. Roughly three and a half hours to go. Three and a half hours without character, promise, or purpose. There was nothing more he had to do, nothing that could possibly interest him. He felt like a traveler between trains in a small town on Sunday, without the wish or hope of seeing a familiar face, smoking cigarette after bitter cigarette. He seemed without identity even to himself until he could be on his way. Idly, he tested the bars on a window. They resisted him without bending. They and the timelock could keep out a regiment, if necessary, until he was ready for help to come in.

He yawned. Only ten minutes had passed. He settled into the chair again, slouched down in its deep cushions so that the wings of the chair shut off his view of the sides. His gaze fell naturally upon a disordered corner by the door. At first he attached no importance to the objects jumbled there. With a feeling of mild confusion and surprise, he recognized them—his canvases, his easel, his paints. He found it hard to believe that he had once been a painter— only months before—and that this room, with the bars and the straps and the needles, had once been the birthplace of still lifes, of affectionate portraits, of sentimental landscapes.

For a moment, the room became ugly and frightening, and David wanted to tear down the bars, cover the straps with the warm, red carpet; to tell Boyle not to come, to invite forgotten friends to a rousing party.

The feeling passed. David's expression became shrewd, purposeful again. His old enemy, time, was trying to discourage him, to break him down in the few hours remaining. If he thought about the experiment much longer, he might lose his nerve before the expedition through time could begin.

He would make himself think about other things. In an old series of reflexes, he set up a fresh canvas on the easel and began to lay out smears of pigment on his palette. He was driving himself, and his movements were clumsy, his choice of colors irrational. He couldn't visualize anything on the expanse of white. He dug his palette knife into a mound of black and laid a glistening jet streak across the canvas.

Critics had once remarked upon his meticulous brushwork, the fineness of detail. On even large expanses of color, he had never used anything but chisel brushes no wider than his wedding ring. Now he spread color in gobs from the palette knife. His hands did as they pleased, as though guided by a spirit outside his own. He felt no more than the infantile delight of smearing.

David looked from his painting to his watch with surprise. The three and a half hours had fled. Boyle would be there at any instant. There was the sound of tires digging through the deep gravel outside. The doctor had arrived.

The fleeting terror, the awe of his surroundings, burst upon him again. He was panting. Footsteps crunched in the gravel.

David closed his eyes and told himself again that no expeditions in human history had been more important than the one he was forcing himself to make. He would die for a moment, explore eternity, revive, and tell the living that every instant they lived was as permanent a part of the universe as the largest constellation. In men's minds, time would cease to be a killer.

The doorbell rang. David lay down on the hard floor and tightened the straps about his ankles, his waist, his shoulders, and his left arm. If convulsions were to be a part of dying, these would keep him from injuring himself. With his free right hand, he worked the hypodermic needle into a vein in his left forearm. The fluid in it would stop his heart. The doorbell rang again.

David twisted his head for one last look around the studio. The door was barred by the timelock. The pulmotor and a second hypodermic syringe—identical to the one that Boyle had driven into the drowned farmer's heart—were in plain view, ready. With these, Dr. Boyle would bring him back to life.

David filled his lungs. He cupped the electric switch in his right hand, drove the air from his lungs, and closed the circuit. A faint tickling in his left arm told him that the syringe had emptied itself into his bloodstream. He didn't look at it, but stared instead at the formless painting on the easel at his feet. The timelock on the door was ticking. Any moment now, Boyle would be crossing the living room and shaking the door.

The telephone jangled. Savagely, David grabbed the cord with his free hand and brought the instrument crashing onto the floor beside him. To die to *that* damn noise!

"Dave," said a voice, tinny and weak in the earpiece inches from David's head. "Dave, this is Boyle." Again from the driveway, the sound of wheels in gravel, this time receding, growing fainter—gone.

David hadn't the strength to turn his head toward the phone. He wanted to lick his lips, but his tongue only quivered feebly. He hardly heard the words piping in the earpiece, was unable to attach meaning to them.

"Listen, I'm over in Rexford," the voice was saying. "It's a premature birth, and I've got to get the kid into an incubator. Can you hold out for a couple of hours..."

David concentrated his dimming consciousness on the painting. Curious, he was thinking, how curious that only now had he realized what it was he had painted. Now, from a distance, the seeming smears blended into a stunning landscape. He tried to smile, a wan salute to his masterpiece.

He admired the Spring-warmed green slope...the pool at its foot, brimming over the boulders of a crude dam...the young lovers swirling bare feet in the pool's crest...the woman's face was the face of an angel...so vivid that her lips seem about to move...

EPISODE TWO
ROME

This is a story about a girl who was raised by her father, who worshipped her father—and then found out he was a terrible hypocrite. This really happened.

It happened the year I was president of the North Crawford Mask and Wig Club. That was the year of the big sorghum and oil scandal down in Barbell, Oklahoma. A man named Fred Lovell was the main crook. Lovell had an eighteen-year-old daughter named Melody, and no wife. And he had a sister in North Crawford. So he sent Melody up to live with his sister until the trouble blew over.

He thought the trouble would blow over. It didn't.

* * *

Melody joined the Mask and Wig Club. She was so beautiful, and we thought it was so important to take her mind off her father's trial, that we gave her a leading part in a play right away. We gave her the part of Bella, a streetwalker with a heart of gold, in *Rome*, by Arthur Garvey Ulm.

There were only four parts in the play: Bella; Ben, the good American soldier; Jed, the bad American soldier; and Bernardo, a cynical Roman policeman. The time was World War II.

Bryce Warmergran got the part of the good soldier, the poet. Bryce was a mother's boy who had been raised in New York City. His mother, a widow, owned the Warmergran Lumber Company, and the Warmergran Lumber Company owned practically every tree and stump in northern New Hampshire. Bryce was in North Crawford for a year to learn all he could about trees. He was a nice, shiny, shy, polite boy.

Bryce had never acted before. All he had done for the club was dip punch during intermissions. I remember what John Sherwood, the electrical contractor, said about Bryce dipping punch. "That job is neither too big nor too little for that boy." That summed up Bryce very well.

John Sherwood was in *Rome*, too. He was the bad soldier. He was six feet four, skinny, broad-shouldered, and the town tomcat. He was famous among the ladies for his dancing ability, his foul mouth, and his barracuda smile. He could also act. He loved to act. He loved to make the ladies in the audience itch and squirm.

I was the cynical policeman. I had to grow a handle-bar mustache.

Rome was directed by Sally St. Coeur.

* * *

Sally called the four of us together in the back room of her gift shop for a first reading of the play. The name of the shop was The Better Mousetrap. Sally had talked to Melody a good deal. We three men were getting our first really close look at the girl.

The thing that impressed me most, aside from her very pretty face, was her posture. She kept her elbows against her sides, her shoulders hunched over, and her hands up against her chest, as though she were scared to death of getting germs. The thing Bryce said he noticed about her was what he called her "purity." He said that, up to the time he saw Melody, he hadn't believed it was possible for a woman to be that pure. What John Sherwood said about her isn't fit to print. What it boiled down to was that women that cold and that ignorant of the facts of life made him sick. The innocence of that girl was an unforgivable attack on all John held dear.

There wasn't any question about Melody's being ignorant and innocent. The first question she asked Sally was, "Excuse me, Miss St. Coeur, but what's a streetwalker?"

"Hold your hats," John whispered to me.

"A streetwalker, dear?" said Sally. "Why, that's a—that's a woman who takes money."

"Oh," said Melody.

"There goes the reputation of every decent female cashier in the world," whispered John.

"Now, about this play—" said Sally, "it only lasted one night on Broadway. But, after reading it over, I realized that the actors and the director were to blame, not the play. It's a magnificent play, and this is a great opportunity for us to give it the performance it deserved and never got."

"Who is Arthur Garvey Ulm?" asked John.

"He's the man who wrote the play."

"I *know* that. I wondered what *else* he'd ever done."

"I—I don't think he's done anything else," said Sally.

"There's a full life for you," said John.

"Can I ask another question?" said Melody.

"Certainly, dear." That was very brave of Sally.

"I've read this whole thing through," said Melody, "and there's several places where it says I'm supposed to kiss different people?"

"Yes?"

Melody shook her head, looked very unhappy. "I got to really *do* that?"

"Uh—yay-uss," said Sally.

"Miss St. Coeur—I promised my daddy I wouldn't never kiss no man except my husband."

John gave an exasperated sigh that sounded like a freight whistle.

Melody turned to him coldly and said, "I suppose you think that's old-fashioned or unsophisticated or something."

"Why no," he said. "I think it's perfectly sacred."

"I can't tell whether you mean it or not."

And then Bryce spoke up. It was the first time I had ever heard him speak up on any subject. He was breathing shallowly, and he'd turned the color of tomato juice. "Miss Lovell—" he said, "any woman who has the courage to hold onto high ideals like that in this day and age is as brave and noble as a woman can be."

Melody was grateful. "Thank you," she said. "I didn't realize there were any men around who would respect a girl with high ideals."

"There are a few," said Bryce.

"There's more of 'em than most people would care to admit," said John.

"Shut up," I told him.

"Dear, about this kissing—" said Sally.

"I just can't do it, Miss St. Coeur—especially with an audience watching."

"Um," said Sally.

"My daddy says kissing folks in public is the most disgusting thing there is." The man who had told her that was under indictment for swindling his neighbors and his country out of six million dollars.

***

"Dear, a play is *not* life," Sally told Melody. "If an actress plays the part of a woman who isn't as good as she might be, that doesn't mean the morals of the actress are really bad."

"How's a woman gonna play an impure part and not have impure thoughts?"

"Good question," said John.

"Surely, dear, you've seen movies or television shows where actresses who lead perfectly respectable private lives—"

"Name one," whispered John.

"I've never seen television," said Melody. "I've never seen a movie. I've never seen a play. Daddy says it's movies and television and books and all that that make the young people's minds so dirty these days." She caught John smirking. She hated him as much as he hated her. "Oh, I see you laughing. I'm used to folks laughing. Daddy told me there'd be folks who'd laugh. 'That's all right—you *let* 'em laugh,' he told me. 'You're gonna get the last laugh, Honeybunch, when you go to Heaven and they go to Hell.'"

***

How we kept on or why we kept on I don't know, but we did. That seems to be the basic rule in amateur theater—keep going, no matter what. The worst thing the Mask and Wig Club ever went ahead with wasn't *Rome*. The worst thing by far was *Oedipus Rex*, by Sophocles. But that is another story. Suffice it to say that the treasurer of the North Crawford Savings and Loan Association had to get up in front of all the depositors wearing a bedsheet, and then tear his eyeballs out on account of he had married his mother by accident.

As far as the Arthur Garvey Ulm play goes, we *did* try to ease Melody out of the cast, but she wouldn't quit. "No," she said. "I've started this, and I'm gonna see it through. My daddy told me, 'Honeybunch, anything you start you finish. The only thing I ask is, don't never do nothing I'd be ashamed of.'"

And Sally got her talked around to where she agreed to kiss Bryce and John and me the way the script said. Only she wasn't going to do it in rehearsals. She would only do it on the night of the performance.

"That's probably a good rule anyway," said Sally. "I'll never forget *La Ronde*."

La Ronde was a play by an Austrian named Arthur Schnitzler. It was a play about how everybody in Vienna was having love affairs with everybody else. The club tried to put on a cleaned-up version of it at one time.

During rehearsals, everybody was kissing everybody else, and the Asiatic flu broke out. We never did get to put on the play. We never could get a flu-free cast.

* * *

How did Melody feel about the grand jury indicting her daddy, and all that? She made a speech about it that first night. Very gently, we were trying to find out what kind of religion, exactly, she and her daddy represented. It turned out that he didn't belong to any church.

"My daddy," she said, "just reads the *Bible* and lives accordingly." And then she started to cry. "He's got the highest morals in Oklahoma. Oh, there's gonna be some people gonna eat some black, greasy crow when that trial comes up. I *know* my daddy, and when the trial begins, the whole world's gonna know my daddy. They're gonna see a saint on a pure white horse. And all the dirty-minded, whisky-drinking, cigarette-smoking, woman-chasing people who accused him falsely will be the ones to go to jail, and I'll laugh and laugh. And all the flags in Barbell will fly, and all the church bells will ring, and the Boy Scouts will have a parade, and the governor of Oklahoma will say, 'I proclaim this day Fred Lovell Day!'"

She pulled herself together. "Let's get on," she said.

"Your mother's dead, is she, dear?" Sally asked.

"She's in Los Angeles, leading a life of sin. Daddy cast her out when I was two." She blew her little nose.

"Cast her out?"

"She was dirty," said Melody, "in both mind and deed."

* * *

Ulm's play starts with a scene on a Roman street corner at night. Bryce Warmergran, the good soldier, sees this streetwalker under a lamppost, and he's so innocent that he doesn't know what she is. She is young and beautiful, and he has been drinking wine for the first time in his life, and he regards her as sacred.

"What flower is this that blooms in the Roman night?" he asks. On top of being a good soldier, he's a poet, too. Bryce read his part very well right from the first. There wasn't any make-believe about it. He was crazy about Melody.

And Melody says back to him, "Night-blooming flowers are very common in Rome. But you have a sensitive face, soldier. Perhaps you will be more clever than most about which one you pick."

And then there's a lot of palaver where Bryce carries on about how flowers shouldn't be picked, how they ought to be left growing wherever they are, so other people can appreciate them, and so forth. And he says that wars are times when people go around tearing up flowers by the roots, and so forth.

The upshot is that she gains self-respect for the first time because a man has spoken to her respectfully for the first time. And Bryce has three months of back combat pay with him, and he gives it all to her without even wanting a kiss. "Don't ask me to explain," he tells her. "One doesn't have to explain one's actions in dreams." He pauses. "In wars." He pauses again. "In life." Ulm has him pause again. "In love," he says, and he drifts off into the night.

* * *

And then along comes John Sherwood, the bad soldier, practically dragging his knuckles on the sidewalk. He is drunk and disorderly, and is smoking a black cigar. He has deserted the army and has made a fortune on the black market. He is carrying a suitcase filled with cigarettes, nylons, and chocolate bars.

Melody is still looking after Bryce, still all luminous with newfound self-respect. And John comes up behind her and says, "You speak English real good, baby."

"What?" she asks.

"I said somebody who talks English as good as you do must have known quite a few Yankee soldiers."

"You heard me talking to that man?"

"I heard you talking to that *boy*. He's a boy, a baby. If you don't know the difference between a boy and a man, I don't know who would."

"I don't know what you mean."

John gives her his famous barracuda smile. And the upshot is that he breaks down her self-respect again, and they go off together.

* * *

The company in Boston that sells us the playbooks and collects royalties was very interested in our production. We were the first amateur group to put on *Rome*. The company wrote me, asked if we were encountering any special difficulties.

I stopped by Sally's store, showed her the letter. "Special difficulties—" she said, "that's ironical, that is."

"They just want to know about things that are Arthur Garvey Ulm's fault," I said. "They don't want to hear about Barbell, Oklahoma."

"I wish *I'd* never heard of it," she said. The play was in its fifth week of rehearsal, had one week to go. And, thanks to Melody, it was putrid. I mean it was really vile.

"Maybe we ought to call it off," I said.

"New Hampshire's depressed enough as it is," she said, "with winter coming on."

The thing was that Melody was absolutely incapable of any character change. The way Ulm had written the play, the main action was what went on in the street-walker's soul, was what she thought of herself after men treated her one way or another. In the little foreword to the play, Ulm said, "In order for *Rome* to come alive, Bella's soul, as sensed by the audience, must be a dazzling kaleidoscope—a kaleidoscope reflected smokily in a mirror in Hell. If Bella leaves out one band of color in the full spectrum of what it means to be a destitute, rootless young woman in a country torn by war, then *Rome* will fail."

I mentioned Ulm's foreword to Sally, asked her if Melody knew what a kaleidoscope was.

"Yes," said Sally. "She also knows what a spectrum is. What she doesn't know is what a woman is."

"You mean what a woman sometimes *has* to be," I said.

"Suit yourself," said Sally.

There was a glum silence. It was late afternoon outside. And Sally suddenly put her hand over her mouth and said, "No, no, no, no!" She was imitating Melody. During rehearsals, whenever we reached a place where Melody was supposed to kiss Bryce or John, that was what she would do.

And Melody wasn't much better than that between kisses. No matter what men said and did to her, she was

Fred Lovell's daughter, who would never do anything to make her daddy ashamed.

"Maybe we should have cast her as Saint Joan of Arc," I said.

Sally snorted, and she asked me, "What makes you think Saint Joan of Arc was full of novocain?"

* * *

But we kept going, no matter what.

Everybody knew his or her lines, anyway, as the case might be. I said to Sally at the final rehearsal before dress rehearsal what somebody always says at the final rehearsal before dress rehearsal: "Well, we've got a play."

"The question is, what's it about?" she said. She had a point. There was Melody up on stage being Melody, and there was Bryce being Bryce, and John being John, and me being me—and somehow we'd all gotten to Rome. And every so often one of us would open his or her mouth, and out would come spooky words that *didn't* have anything to do with anything, *words* from outer space, words from another world, the words of Arthur Garvey Ulm.

The rehearsal was still going on when I said we had a play. I wasn't in that particular scene. As it happened, I sat down next to one of John's many girlfriends. Her name was Marty. She was a waitress from South Crawford. Like about half of John's admirers, she'd had her nose broken at one time or another. It seems to me that about half of his girls were named Marty, too.

This particular Marty dug her elbow into my ribs, and she said, "That Bryce Warmergran is a hot sketch, ain't he?" She was laughing her head off. She thought it was supposed to be a funny play.

And Bryce was funny, too, God help us. He was crazy about that touch-me-not, that plaster of Paris marshmallow sundae, that Melody. And he prowled around her in sort of a Groucho Marx squat, looked up at her with very gooey goo-goo eyes. That was how he carried out Ulm's instructions in the script, which said, "Ben, the good soldier, has a soul nearly as mercurial as that of the girl, for remember: he is a poet, and the passions of a poet, by definition, can never be predicted, can never be controlled."

Marty asked me if Melody was worried about her father's trial. I replied that nobody knew when the trial would be. The government had teams of investigators in Barbell, according to the papers, and it looked as though it would take them years to find out exactly what Fred Lovell had done and how he'd done it.

"As far as Melody's concerned," I said, "her father is sin-proof. She can't conceive of his doing wrong, so she isn't worried at all." I shrugged. "And who knows— maybe he *will* get off."

"Yeah," said Marty. "Seems like everybody but Eichmann gets off these days. Is this Lovell walking around, or locked up, or what?"

"I imagine he's out on bail or something," I said.

"They all are," she said.

And that was when Fred Lovell himself came into the auditorium.

* * *

I knew right away who he was. His pictures had been in the papers and on television many times. He was a chunky man, moon-faced, with a button nose and a high forehead. He had steel-rimmed spectacles with lenses the size of quarters. He had on a very boxy, double-breasted suit that looked as though it were made out of splintered plywood. He only had one expression, and that was sort of a Queen Victoria scowl.

I went to meet him. His breast pocket was crammed with fountain pens, and one lapel twinkled like the Milky Way. The lapel had the emblems of at least a dozen fraternal and service organizations pinned to it, and I wouldn't have been surprised to see a Dr. Pepper bottlecap there, too. What impressed me most about Fred Lovell, though, was the heavy perfume of booze.

I greeted him very loudly, so everybody would be warned. "Mr. Lovell! What a pleasant surprise!" I said. "We had no idea you were coming!"

The houselights came up. The play stopped. Melody shrieked for joy from the stage. She came running to her daddy, threw her arms around him. I wondered what she would say when she smelled all that booze on him.

"Oh, Daddy, Daddy, Daddy—" she said, "you've got too much aftershave lotion on again."

***

Sally said we might as well start from the first again, so we did. "Mr. Lovell," she said, "if you'll sit down somewhere—I think you're going to be very proud of your daughter."

"Always was," he said. "Never had any reason not to be."

There were only six people in the audience and three hundred empty chairs. Lovell surveyed the situation, looked a little like W. C. Fields trying to find a straight pool cue. And then he picked the seat I had just vacated, the one next to John Sherwood's broken-nosed girlfriend.

"What are you in this play?" he asked her.

"I'm not in it," she said.

"Then how come you're all painted up?" he wanted to know.

A few seconds before the houselights went out again, a young stranger tiptoed into the auditorium, took a seat at the very back. His hair was long, and he was all unbuttoned, but I assumed he was a G-man. I thought he was following Fred Lovell, making sure he didn't get away.

* * *

I was in the first scene, so I had to be up onstage. I didn't have anything to say. I just walked through twice, looking cynical. I was in the wings with John Sherwood. Melody was out under the lamppost, waiting for the curtain to go up.

"Mmm *mmm!*" John said to me. "Man, that's sure a lot of woman out there." He smacked his lips. "I can hardly wait for that kiss on Friday night! Yum, yum, yum, boy—that ought to be about the best kiss a man could ever have."

"No need to make fun of her just because she doesn't have a broken nose," I said.

"You show me a woman with a broken nose," he said, "and I'll show you a woman who thinks it's important to make a man happy." He shook his head, looked at Bryce, who was waiting for his cue on the other side. "Now there's a boy who just might get killed by the miracle of that Friday night kiss."

"Killed?" I said.

"I doubt if he's got any immunity to any disease at all," said John. "He's never been exposed to *anything*."

And then the curtain went up.

Melody swiveled around some in the circle of light under the lamppost. Sally had told her to do that. Melody had asked her, "Why?" Melody wasn't in costume, but she was swinging a big, shiny, patent leather purse on a long strap. No matter how pure her thoughts might be, it was obvious to anybody but Bryce Warmergran what she was meant to be.

There was a loud "Haw!" out of John's girlfriend. She loved that play.

And then, before anybody onstage had said anything, Fred Lovell gave a terrible groan. "Bring down that curtain!" he roared.

* * *

The curtain crashed down. The houselights came up. I, as club president, went out to argue with that crazy man. He was on his feet. He was purple. The unbuttoned young stranger in the trench coat was standing, too.

"This filthy play is off!" said Lovell.

"Sir?" I said.

"My sweet daughter—" he said. He choked up. "The most perfect thing in my life, the only perfect thing in my life, and you got her under a lamppost, swinging a purse! I am not delighted. I am not delighted at all!"

Melody came out from backstage, scared stiff.

"You're getting out of here!" Lovell told her.

"We're going back to Barbell, Daddy?"

"You're going back to your aunt's house."

"Can't I come with you?"

"Not yet, honey. Later on. Meanwhile, you get away from these people, and you *keep* away from 'em! They're no good for you. You hear?"

"I hear." Melody wasn't about to argue. She took her father's arm, and the two of them marched out.

Right after they left, the young stranger left, too. He slammed the door.

I turned to Sally. "What's going through *your* filthy mind?" I asked her.

"He was crying," said Sally.

"His eyes looked dry to me."

"Who are you talking about?" she said.

"Lovell," I said. "Tartuffe." Tartuffe is a hypocrite in a French play we put on one time.

"I was talking about the young man in the trench coat," she said.

"G-men," I told her, "never cry."

* * *

The next evening, the story was in all the papers: Fred Lovell was a fugitive from justice. He had jumped bail. Right after taking Melody back to her aunt, he'd headed for the Canadian border, crossed it, gotten to Montreal. In Montreal he'd hopped a plane for Brazil.

His eighty-thousand-dollar bail was forfeited, the papers said. It wasn't Lovell's money. It had been scratched up by ordinary citizens of Barbell who still believed in him.

There was another nasty little story on the side, too, with pictures. The pictures were of Fred Lovell's mistress, a very fancy young woman with eyelashes like buggy whips, with long diamond earrings, with piles of champagne-colored hair. She had been seen in New Orleans, boarding a plane for Brazil.

"What does this do to the play?" my wife asked me at supper.

"There's nothing left to *do* to the play," I said.

"I'm scared to ask the real question."

"What's it do to Melody?" I said. "God only knows. Sally's tried to call her all day long, but she won't come to the phone. She's locked up in her bedroom."

"Is the door locked from the outside or the inside?"

"Good question. From the inside."

The telephone rang. I answered it. It was John Sherwood. He wanted to know if there was going to be a dress rehearsal that night.

"What do you think?" I asked him.

"Well, I've got one idea," he said. "The posters are all up, the publicity's been going on for weeks, and the tickets are practically sold. We've got a couple hundred bucks tied up in the set and costumes—"

"You are not telling me the news, John."

"Suppose my girlfriend took over the part of Bella," he said.

"Marty?" I said. "Can she act?"

"Could Melody act?" said John. "At least Marty knows what the play's about. She's seen practically every rehearsal. If I worked with her for the next three days, come Friday, she'd be ready to go on."

"It's worth a try," I said. "I'll call everybody and tell them there'll be a dress rehearsal tonight, as planned."

"The play must go on," said John.

"Or something," I said.

* * *

When I got back to the auditorium that night, the young stranger was in the back row again. "May I ask you a question?" I said.

"Go ahead."

"Maybe you're not supposed to answer, and maybe I'm not supposed to ask—but are you a G-man?"

"Do I look like a G-man?"

"Not close up," I said.

"Then I leave you to your own conclusions," he said.

"If you are following Fred Lovell, I hate to tell you, but your bird has flown."

"That's the breaks," he said.

That was the end of the conversation. I went up front, minding my own business. The rehearsal hadn't started yet, but John's girl was under the lamppost, warming up.

"How's she gonna be?" I asked Sally.

"There's going to be a police raid for the first time in the history of the North Crawford Mask and Wig Club," said Sally.

I saw what she meant. Marty was going to turn Arthur Garvey Ulm's masterpiece into a really rugged, dirty, low-down play.

"Has Bryce seen her yet?" I said.

"He turned snow white and disappeared. I think he's cowering in the basement somewhere."

And then Melody walked in. Her eyes were red, and there were circles under them, but she was very calm. She had made herself up with false eyelashes, heavy mascara, circles of rouge on her cheeks. And her mouth, as they say in books, was a scarlet slash.

That girl radiated so much tragedy and so much dignity that everyone got out of her way. Marty, when she saw Melody, slunk away from the lamppost without a word.

Melody got up onstage, looked out at us over the footlights, closed her eyes for a long time, opened them again. "Shall we begin?" she said.

* * *

Great God—what a performance that was! Melody was ten times life size. People in the audience sobbed out loud as Melody represented every kind of female from the Little Match Girl to Mary Magdalene.

And when it was time to kiss, that girl kissed. The first time she kissed Bryce, he came reeling into the wings with only the whites of his eyes showing. The first time she kissed John, he made his exit like a man of the world. But when he was out of sight of the audience, he went down on his hands and knees.

When Melody came off at the end of the first act, I caught her in my arms. "You're the greatest actress this club ever had!"

"I'm like her!" she said. "I'm trash! I'm garbage!" She got loose from me, went over to John, threw her arms around his neck. "I'm what you need, and you're what I need," she said. "Let's you and me run off," she said.

That was fine with John. "Sure, baby," he said. "You and me—you bet, you bet."

The door to the audience flew open, and in came the young stranger. He looked wilder than anybody. He pushed John aside, and he put his arms around Melody. "I love you more than any woman has ever been loved! I'm not going to ask you to marry me. You *have* to marry me. There is no choice! It *has* to be!"

"Wait 'til J. Edgar Hoover hears about this," I said.

"What's he got to do with it?" he said.

"You're the most unbuttoned G-man I ever heard of," I said.

"I'm no G-man," he said.

"Who are you?" I said.

"I am a playwright," he said, "named Arthur Garvey Ulm."

EPISODE THREE
EDEN BY THE RIVER

When the hunter passed them in the woods, the boy and the girl pretended not to have anything to do with each other, pretended to be on separate walks, looking for birds. The hunter glanced at each of them with just enough whimsy to let them know that he wasn't fooled, that he knew and liked young lovers when he saw them.

When he was gone, the two resumed their game with the stone.

The boy was seventeen, tall, still growing—as graceless as a homemade stepladder. His wrists were thick, his shoulders still narrow. His feet and hands were big, and his legs were long, sweeping him through the woods with the gait of a man on stilts. His face was the face of a sweet, grave child, surprised at being up so high in the air for so long.

He stepped out of the path and pressed his back against a tree. He was breathing quickly, happy and alert, waiting for the girl to kick the stone.

The stone was as small and blue as a robin's egg. It lay on damp moss on the path. The boy and the girl, taking turns, had kicked it a mile into the woods from the driveway where they'd found it.

Now, fifty feet beyond the stone, the path ended at a river.

The girl was nineteen, small, mature, and silkily muscular. Her lovely features twisted in humorless concentration as she walked up to the stone, took aim, and kicked it.

As the stone skittered down the path, the boy dashed after it, floundering, flapping. He feinted, bobbed, blocked an imaginary opponent, and kicked the stone again.

The stone flew low and fast, hit the river, and sank, twinkling dimly, quickly out of sight.

The boy turned and smiled at the girl in triumph, as though the world had never seen manly strength like his before.

Her eyes didn't disappoint him. They were filled with love and admiration. "You shouldn't have kicked it so far," she said. "Not all the way to the river. I wanted it. I wanted to keep it."

"We can kick another one home," he said. "You can keep that one."

"It wouldn't be as good," she said. "No stone will ever be quite that good."

"A stone's a stone," he said.

"That's just like a man to say that," she said. "It takes a woman to see what should be saved and what should be thrown away." She sat on a flat rock on the riverbank and patted the place beside her. "Sit here. It's dry."

He considered the place, then chose another a dozen feet away from her, a sunless, spongy patch, spiked with reed stumps.

"Are you really comfortable over there?" she said. "Wouldn't you rather be in the sunshine?"

"Fine," he said. "Really." He found twisted pleasure in being uncomfortable, in keeping away from her.

"Eden must have like this before the apple," she said. "Simple. Clean."

"Yup," he said.

When they were alone together, she was the one who embroidered the moments with words of affection. His replies were grunts, inattentive, barely civil. His thoughts were undefined, a hazy sense of pride and peace.

"Just two people, and the animals and the plants," she said. "So quiet." She took off her shoes and stretched her legs to wet her toes in the river. "And all we say is being said for the first time. And it just has to do with us," she said. "There isn't anybody else anywhere."

"Um," he said. He looked away from her pink toes and the curves of her calves indifferently. He took a knife from his pocket and peeled the bark from a sapling. "I guess she's wondering where we are," he said.

"We're where we should be," she said.

"I don't know what kind of a story we can make up to tell her what got into us," he said. "Running off like this—kicking an old stone like a couple of crazy kids."

"We don't have to make up stories," she said. "We aren't children. Today's the day we stop being children."

He shook his head wonderingly. "Crazy! I didn't any more think this was going to happen than fly to the moon."

"I like things that just happen," she said. She didn't seem at all surprised or puzzled by what had happened.

The boy frowned, pondering the mystery. "It was the craziest thing ever," he said. "I was just trying to keep out of everybody's way, standing out there in the driveway, not thinking about anything. And I saw the stone. Then you came out, and I kicked the stone, and you kicked it—"

"And here we are," she said. "I was watching you out the window a long time."

"You were?" he said.

"Didn't you feel me looking down at you?" she said. "I can always feel it when people look at me."

He stopped whittling and reddened, thinking of her looking at him secretly. "I thought you were off on another world somewhere," he said. "With all the stuff you have to do and think about—"

"I was looking at you," she said. "So tall, so handsome."

"I'm funny looking," he said.

"No you're not," she said.

"You're the only one who doesn't think so," he said.

She tossed her head, impatient with his self-pity.

He was ashamed. He covered his shame by standing briskly and dusting his hands. "We'd better get on back," he said.

"I'm not ready to go yet," she said.

"Well, whenever you're ready," he said.

"It seems like there ought to be things we should say to each other," she said.

He shrugged. "I guess we're pretty well talked out by now," he said. "You'd think we'd have said everything there was to say to each other a couple of hundred times by now."

She looked out at the river, and her eyes widened with a big thought. "Maybe if you kissed me," she said distantly, "that would say everything that needs to be said. Would you mind that?"

He was startled. "Why no—I wouldn't mind," he said. "You mean *now*?"

"Please," she said. "I think it would be nice."

"Why, sure, sure," he said. He shambled over to her, his hands limp before him, like flippers. Looking down on her, he was overwhelmed by a feeling of idiocy, grinning, shuffling his feet—as though a practical joke were in progress. "On the forehead?"

"That would be fine," she said.

He kissed her lightly on the forehead, the kiss like a falling dry leaf. Before he could pull away, she pressed her cheek against his. Her cheek was hot, and his cheek burned as he went back to his sunless, spongy, spikey spot.

"OK?" he said.

"Perfect," she said. "That's the first time you've ever kissed me. Why is that?"

"Oh, why heck—" he said. His hands worked in air. "I mean...well, for heaven's sake...it just isn't that kind of a thing, is all."

Her expression hadn't changed since he'd kissed her. She still stared wide-eyed at the river. "You know what I think?" she said.

"No," he said.

"I think almost everything is that kind of thing," she said. She stood and stepped into her shoes, smiling possessively at him all the while. "And now that I've said that," she said, "it really *is* time to get back."

She seemed relieved about something.

On the walk home, she was serene and unresponsive.

The boy kicked another stone, a white one, down the path. He danced around it challengingly before her eyes. She paid no attention, and he felt foolish.

He kicked the stone into the underbrush, dug his hands deep into his pockets, and hunched his shoulders, trying to find thoughts of his own.

He wondered if she was annoyed with him for not having said more about how he liked her, for not having thought of the kiss himself. Once before, when she'd told him she loved another man, she'd expected him to talk. And he'd said almost nothing. He'd been eager to say things. But whatever there was to say had fled and left him dumb.

They met the hunter again. The hunter kept his eyes down demurely until he reached the boy. Then he looked up at the boy suddenly and winked. The wrinkles in the hunter's face formed a whirlpool around the one salacious eye.

* * *

The boy and the girl were met at the door of the big white house by a lean woman in her late forties. She was dressed for a wedding. Behind her, in the twilight of the house, people were polishing silver, wiping glasses, putting flowers in vases, dusting dark woodwork that already shone. Somewhere a vacuum cleaner snuffled under carpets and bumped into baseboards.

"Where have you been?" said the woman unhappily. She twisted a handkerchief in her hands. "The guests will be here in less than an hour."

"I've got plenty of time, Aunt Mary," said the girl. "Everything's all laid out. I've tried it on dozens of times, and it's all perfect."

"If your father and mother were alive," said the woman, "you wouldn't have treated *them* this way—simply walking off without a word."

"It's something I had to do," said the girl. She looked at her aunt levelly. "I just had to, Aunt Mary, or I wouldn't have done it."

"You could have *told* me," said the woman.

"I didn't know it was going to happen until it happened," said the girl. "I'll go now and get ready." She brushed past her aunt and went up the stairs two steps at a time.

"Heyden!" her aunt called after her. "It's time you learned some responsibility toward others!" She turned her attention to the boy. "You'd better get ready, too."

"All right."

"You know what you're to say?" she said.

"Yes," he said.

"Clear your throat before you say it, to be sure your voice won't crack."

"It won't."

Her face relaxed as she looked at him. Her anxiety was replaced by tenderness. "Oh dear—that's when I'm going to cry," she said. "When you speak up, I just won't be able to stand it." Tears formed on the rims of her eyes. "Nobody will," she said. "You standing there so straight—"

"Yup," he said, embarrassed for them both. He tried to get past her, but she caught his sleeve.

"Do you know what it means—what an awfully moving thing it is you're going to say?" she said.

The question and the tears annoyed him. "Yeah, sure—I guess," he said.

"Do you *really*?" she said intensely.

"Yeah—yes, yes, yes!" he said. "I tell you yes!"

She let go of his sleeve and took a step backward. "Why are you so angry all of a sudden?" she said.

He flapped his arms in irritable confusion. "I dunno!" he said. "People tell me to get in the way, get out of the way; say something, shut up; stand up, sit down." He waved the wedding straight to hell. "I dunno! I guess it's a woman's thing! I'll be glad when it's over." He walked away from her. "When it's over," he said, "maybe I'll be able to do a little living of my own again.

* * *

The boy, the groom, and the best man were in the damp cellar of the big white house. The shoes of the wedding guests scuffed overhead.

The groom opened the lid on the water meter, read the meter judiciously, and closed the lid with a snap. "Aren't you supposed to be upstairs?" he said to the boy.

"Search me," said the boy. "If I'm not supposed to be down here, some woman will come and pull me by the ears to where I'm supposed to be. I'd rather stay down here with you guys."

"We aren't much company," said the best man.

"What guy is at a time like this?" said the boy.

The groom smiled. "You sound like *you're* the one who's getting married," he said. He held out his hand to the best man. "Let's have that flask again."

The best man handed the groom a silver flask, and the groom drank. He drank with his eyes open, looking at the boy.

The camaraderie of the moment warmed the boy. Here at least he could be at ease with two men he knew and liked—at ease away from the women's mysteries. There were no demands on him here, no emotions to confuse him. "I'd like a drink, too, if you don't mind," he said.

The groom started to offer the flask without a thought. Then he pulled it back. "Wait," he said playfully, "that would be contributing to the delinquency of a minor."

"Worse than that," said the best man, "it would destroy his health."

"Why yes," said the groom. "He's still got growing to do. We can't let him jeopardize his physique. That physique is going to make some woman very happy someday."

The next moment seemed to last forever, as the boy's extended hand closed on nothing.

He saw now that the groom was no friend at all—saw how ugly he was, with teeth too big and white, with lips too thick, with eyes too greedy. And on and on the groom's grin went—radiant with conceit and derision.

The feel of the girl's cheek in the woods came back to the boy. His own cheek burned again. Suddenly he wanted to tell the groom about the walk in the woods, the quiet time by the river, the kiss. He wanted to curl his lip and tell the groom that he'd never know love like that in a million years.

But he didn't say anything. He stared stonily.

"It was just a gag," said the groom genially. "Gee whiz, boy—don't look so down in the mouth, like you lost your best friend. I thought *you* were kidding *us* about the drink." He took the boy's hand and shook it manfully. "Heeeeeey—we can't be mad at each other today."

The groom was a friend again, affectionate, good looking.

The boy looked away, bewildered by the noisy emotions that had been coming and going all day like summer thunderstorms. "I was just kidding about being sore," he said.

The lean woman called down the stairway for the boy to come up. "Hurry!" she said.

"Wish me luck," said the groom, letting go of the boy's hand.

"Good luck," said the boy.

"Thanks," said the groom. "I'll need it."

* * *

The boy was walking with the girl again. And this time she was on his arm.

His heart was beating like a fire alarm. He was ready to talk now, to tell her how he loved her. The words were ready, bursting his soul.

But her hand was cold, and her arm was as still as dry sticks. Her face was frozen in a smile that had nothing to do with him.

He was too late. He had missed his chance when they were in Eden by the river.

He was alone, all alone.

He left her and sat down. His mind was blank, sensitive only to masses of sound and color.

"Who gives this woman in marriage?" said the minister.

The boy stood. "I—her brother—do," he said.

EPISODE FOUR
SUCKER'S PORTFOLIO

Everybody has the itch to buy what I sell, because what I sell is advice on how to get richer, *probably*, and advice on what stocks and bonds to buy or sell—and when. It's expert advice, and I study hard to make it that way. But, good as my advice is, not everybody can be a customer, because not everybody has venture capital—money for the stock market and me.

More people have venture capital than are talking about it, and it's my job, if I care to go on eating, to discover these close-mouthed ones and convince them that they would be shrewd to accept my help. And they would be, too. But, America being what it is, it's a nightmare trying to guess who has venture capital and who doesn't.

It never occurred to me to talk about building a portfolio—accumulating a bonanza in securities—to the ragged, foul-mouthed old man who used to sell papers outside my apartment. But when he died, police found $58,000 in venture capital in his mattress. Worse—

before I could rally from the shock, his heir had ventured the whole wad on a Florida motel.

Clothes furnish no clues. A Homburg hat, a banker's gray suit, a regimental tie, and highly polished black shoes are no more indications that a man has venture capital than the shape of his ears. I know. I wear a Homburg hat, a banker's gray suit, a regimental tie, and highly polished black shoes.

So—finding customers is pretty much a lottery, and they're likely to come from anywhere and look like anything.

I was inherited by one of my customers, and he is the most conservative-looking young man I've ever met. I didn't think I could interest him in any investments that were even remotely speculative—ones that might go up or down fast, but probably up. But, after I'd made his $20,000 portfolio as stable and conservative as possible, he threw away $10,000 of it, and I'm still looking for signs of regret.

His name is George Brightman. I was inherited by him from his adoptive parents, lovely people who were among my first customers. Shortly after I got their portfolio shipshape, they lost their lives in an automobile accident, and I went on taking care of the portfolio in the name of their adopted son and heir, George.

I take pride in my work, and I feel especially affectionate toward my early efforts. The Brightman portfolio was a nice job—balanced and strong. In its own way, it was a work of love, because the Brightmans wanted George to have it someday, and they adored George. Well, the time for George to get it came sooner than anyone expected, and it made me sick when he began to dynamite the small but neat financial edifice we'd built for him.

George was a client of mine for six months before I met him. He was a divinity student at the University of Chicago, and the business we did was by correspondence and long-distance telephone calls.

His parents had told me what a clean, kind, splendid young chap he was, working his way through divinity school; and his letters and telephone conversations gave me no reason to think otherwise. I *did* think he was maybe a little too lighthearted and trusting about his financial affairs—but his financial affairs were in the hands of an honest man, fortunately, so he could afford to tell me to do what I pleased with his $20,000. Sometimes his responses to my questions and suggestions were so lackadaisical that I wondered if he cared at all about the portfolio, or had the vaguest idea of what it was or how it worked. Then he stopped being lackadaisical.

The first indication I had of the change was a letter from George, saying he was coming home for a week, and demanding $519.29. At first glance, the letter looked like a forgery, and I suspected that some confidence man had seen the wonderful possibility of going through George's pockets while his head was in the clouds. George's handwriting, as I knew it, was as regular and quietly powerful as slow rollers on the sea before a steady wind. The writing in demand of $519.29 was ragged and choppy.

It was only when I compared the letter with some of George's earlier ones that I saw they were all written by the same hand. The steady rollers had been hit by a squall.

***

"I'm George Brightman," he said gently, stepping into my small office.

"I think I might have guessed," I said. "I saw a lot of snapshots of you when I worked with your parents. And I caught a glimpse of you at the funeral."

"I didn't feel much like meeting anyone then."

"Everybody understood."

He was remarkably small for a man, about five feet four inches tall, I'd say. His face wasn't the calm, bright, amiable moon remembered from the snapshots. And when I'd seen it at the funeral, of course, it had been distorted by grief. The face I saw now was restless and excited, a little wild—in contrast with his dark-gray flannel suit and black tie.

I'd looked forward to a pleasant, leisurely chat with him, but he was in a great hurry about something.

"Where's my money?" he said.

I handed him my personal check for the amount he'd asked for. I pressed my palms together, pursed my lips judiciously, and leaned back, the image of an expert. "Now then, that money is the proceeds from the sale of a hundred shares of Nevada Mining and Exploration," I said. "This leaves your portfolio some-what unbalanced, weakened in natural resources. In my opinion—"

"Well, thanks for everything," said George. "You do whatever's best." He started to leave.

"Listen! Wait!" I said. "We got a thousand dollars for Nevada Mining, so you've got a cash surplus beyond that check of about $480. Now, there's a very fine, small but old and well-run zinc firm that we might be smart to put your $480 into. That would restore some of the balance we've lost, and—"

"Could I have it?"

"The stock in the zinc company?"

"The cash surplus," said George. "The $480."

"George," I said evenly, "may I ask what for?"

"Maybe I'll tell you later," said George, his eyes shining. "It *is* my money, isn't it?"

"It's your money, George. Don't let anybody tell you any different. But—"

"And if I want more, I just tell you to sell something. Isn't that the way it works?"

"Like a dollar watch, George," I said wretchedly. "But—"

"Good. Then you can write me a check for the…the cash surplus." The term pleased him.

I wrote the check slowly. "Maybe it isn't any of my business, George," I said, "but you haven't come across a clean-cut stranger who wants to double your money for you, have you?"

"When the right time comes, you'll hear all about it," said George.

"Then it'll be too late," I said, but he was gone.

*　*　*

I'm no artist, but I honestly believe my business is a lot like painting. It drives me crazy to see a lopsided portfolio, just the way it hurts an artist to see a painting that isn't put together right. After George's raid on his portfolio, which was like cutting a hole in a painting, I couldn't think about anything else. And I couldn't get it out of my head that he—*we*—were being swindled. Before the afternoon was over, I'd convinced myself that I had a holy mandate to mind George's business. All of it.

I called the YMCA and found that he was staying there—of course. When he came to the phone, he sounded even more excited than he'd been in my office.

"We ought to get together for a business talk as soon as possible," I said. "What about supper?"

"Not tonight, not tonight," he said. "Not tonight of all nights. I don't feel like eating anyway."

"Lunch tomorrow?"

"Yes. All right, fine."

I named a restaurant where we would meet. "George," I said casually, "I've been thinking about your portfolio." What I'd been thinking about it was that, if someone was tempting him with prospects of huge profits in a hurry, it was up to me to tempt him into some highly speculative propositions where he had at least a small chance of winning. "If you can possibly hang on to the money you got this afternoon, just until our talk tomorrow, I think I could show you a way to invest it so that you might realize, in a very short time, an increase of—"

"Talk to me about it tomorrow," said George. "My mind is too full now to think about investments."

"Um," I said. "Well—you *will* hang on to the money until tomorrow, eh?"

"Can't," said George, and he hung up.

* * *

I spent a fitful night, trying to imagine what it was that cost $519.29, would be delivered after nightfall, and would excite a divinity student.

I called the YMCA a dozen times in the morning, and was told each time, until noon, that George was resting and couldn't come to the phone.

At noon he agreed to come to the phone, and I could hear the sounds of his steps echoing down the hall as he approached. His footfalls sounded like the slaps of a wet washrag.

"Uh?" said George. His voice was the quack of a duck.

"George?"

"Uh."

"How was the night of nights?"

"Uh."

"Lunch, George—in an hour?"

"Uh."

"George, are you all right?"

"Only God," mumbled George, "could give a man a headache like this."

"We could call off lunch, I suppose. What is it— some virus thing?"

"Sin," said George thickly. "I'll come. I've got to talk to you."

* * *

I knew without asking that the money was gone and that no satisfaction had been received for it—a thousand dollars out the window. I couldn't help feeling pleased, in a twisted way, as I waited in the restaurant for George. He'd bought something, anyway—a good, stiff lesson in economics that he wouldn't forget. It could have been much worse, I thought. He still had $19,000 to hang on to for dear life.

When George walked into the restaurant and peered around for me, his eyes looked like dying fires in the back of a cave. Whoever had taken him to the cleaners had gotten him drunk—a trick I would have considered impossible.

"Where'd you go last night, George?" I said lightheartedly.

"Never mind," he said desolately, and throughout the meal, which he couldn't eat, he hardly said a word.

"You said you had to talk to me?" I coaxed gently.

"I've got to think it out first," he said. "I've got to get it straight in my mind."

"Take your time, take your time," I said. And to make the time pass I spoke interestingly, I thought, about men who had lost their money to swindlers of one sort or another, and who had been doubly foolish in not going to the police about it. "That's how the con men stay in business," I said. "A guy feels so stupid after he's been taken that he doesn't want to let anybody know how stupid he was." I watched George carefully for some flicker of interest.

"Oh well," said George apathetically.

"Oh well?" I said indignantly. "Swindlers take honest people for millions of dollars a year. It's up to people with some guts to turn them in."

George shrugged. "'It is easier for a camel to go through the eye of a needle than for a rich man to enter into the kingdom of God.' Maybe swindlers are doing people a favor."

I was stunned. "George! Let's be practical."

"I thought I was being."

"Well there's certainly some middle ground between being stone broke and being filthy rich, George. I mean, after all, the time is going to come when you're going to be raising a family, and you'll certainly want to give your children certain advantages that cost money. A comfortable home, good schooling, plenty of healthful food. Those things are important to a child."

"That *is* true, isn't it?" said George with sudden intensity.

"If you hadn't been raised in a comfortable home, if your parents hadn't been able to help with your college education, you would have been an entirely different person, George. Those things matter."

"I know," said George gravely. "I'm learning. If I hadn't been adopted as a baby, if I'd been left in the orphanage—" His eyes widened. "There but for the grace of God, go I."

I was delighted. "So you see, George—you've got to take an interest in your portfolio and not do anything foolish with it, because it really belongs to your children. Now, as I told you yesterday, your portfolio is weak in natural resources, and I thought we might sell part of the chemicals, and—"

George stood. "Please," he said apologetically, "some other time. I'm feeling pretty woozy. I better go back to my room and lie down." He reached into his pocket for his billfold.

"No, no, George. This is on me."

"Thanks. Nice of you," said George. He'd taken something from his pocket and was looking at it with something close to nausea. It was a plastic swizzle stick. He broke it vengefully, dropped the pieces into an ashtray, smiled wanly, and fled.

Written on the swizzle stick was a name that must have struck George with horrible irony: Club Joy.

* * *

All was right with the world, I thought, and I expected no more trouble from George. George had learned some important things, and I had helped to teach him. The thought made me happy, and I whistled at my work through most of the afternoon.

I was whistling as I locked up my office, when the telephone rang. "Oh!" I said cheerily, "It's *you*, George.

You sound much better. A hundred percent recovered, I'd say."

"Yes, thank you," said George politely. "I wonder if you could tell me something."

"Glad to."

"How much was my portfolio worth before I sold some of it?"

"To the penny, George?"

"Please."

"Well—I'll have to do some figuring. Hold on." Five minutes later, I was able to give him the figures. "As of closing this afternoon, you were worth $19,021.50. With the cash you got yesterday, $20,021.50."

"And half of that would be—?"

"Well, let's see. Two into twenty goes ten...mmm. That'd be $10,010.75."

"Less $480.71 would be—?"

"Uh—$9,530.04, George. Why?"

"I want you to sell enough securities to get me that amount, please. Use your own discretion."

"George!"

"Can you do it tomorrow?"

"George—what are you up to?"

"If I cared to discuss it, I would," said George coolly.

"George," I said pleadingly, "you said you'd tell me what was going on when the right time came. There never was a righter time than now."

"Sorry," said George. "I'm afraid the right time will never come now. I'll come for the money tomorrow afternoon. Good-bye."

* * *

The Club Joy was under the city streets. I found a smoke-filled bubble blown in the muck between the sewers and the subway.

"Have to check your coat and hat, sir," said the hat-check girl, as I stood on the threshold of the Club Joy, in desperate search for George.

She was a pretty thing, tiny but fierce, blinking up at me with large brown eyes through the haze of hysterical jazz, blood, sweat, and tears coming from the main room. Her hair was bleached as white as a snowdrift, and rhinestone icicles hung from her ears. Her dress was cut so low that, from where I stood, she seemed to be wearing little more than the half door of her booth.

She caressed my Homburg and Chesterfield as she hung them up. "Just like Walter Pidgeon or an ambassador or something," she said. Her fingertips lingered in my palm for a moment as she handed me the brass check.

I started to ask her if she'd seen anyone fitting George's description, but I changed my mind. If someone at the Club Joy had gotten George into $10,000 worth of trouble, I reasoned, it might be unwise—suicide, that is—to show curiosity about George or the nature of his trouble.

The main room of the Club Joy confirmed this. It was joyless, populated with vicious drunks and sullen drunks, and a few men as sober as tombstones, cold and white faced and silent, watching everything in the blue mirror behind the bar. They watched me.

I ordered a drink and looked around casually for George. He wasn't there. I looked casually but many noticed and didn't seem to like it—especially the white-faced men.

I didn't plan to drink much, but in the nightmare of the Club Joy there was nothing to do but drink. Drinking was a physical necessity for those who weren't born numb. My whole system cried out for anesthesia if I were to stay any length of time, and I began to understand how George had come by his crashing hangover.

Two hours later, at midnight, George still hadn't appeared. But there was one important development: I'd come uncoupled from truth and was as tough as they came—a ruthless private eye, out to save George. With baleful eyes that had seen everything, I sized up people as they came in; a good many of them looked away uneasily.

I turned to the sodden fat man on the stool next to mine. "Can't imagine what happened to my buddy," I said craftily. "Supposed to meet me here. You seen him?

Real little guy, with big brown eyes, dark-gray suit, black tie."

"Yeah, I know the one. Nah, hasn't been in t'night."

"You know him?"

"Saw him las' night. That's the only time." He nodded to himself. "Yeah—the kid looks like he don't know his elbow fr'm third base. I know, I know. The one that's so hot for li'l Jackie."

"Jackie?"

"Hatcheck girl. Your pal sat here all las' night, lookin' at 'er in the mirror. Sure couldn't drink."

"Oh?"

"Bartender kept rushin' him to drink more or let somebody else have his stool, and the kid got pretty boozed up."

"Alone?"

"Yeah—'til he took Jackie home. Sure can't tell by lookin' who's after what, can you? Kid looked like he ought to be a minister to me."

* * *

It was no trick getting to take Jackie home. It seemed to be a custom of the house, and I was the best-dressed man in it—at a walkaway.

My recollections of the ride home and what followed are fuzzy. My intentions were perfectly honorable, I know that. I think my plan was to discover, without falling into it myself, what sort of trap she'd caught George in. The plan was crafty, whatever it was.

I dozed frequently in the taxi and caught only snatches of Jackie's conversation, which was bright and phony, brittle as glass. She pulled out all the stops for me: she was lonesome and helpless and poor, and had been raised in a tough orphanage, and had never been happy or understood.

My next recollection was of sitting on a couch in her apartment, trying to keep my eyes open, while she mixed a drink in the kitchen. But my eyes closed, and I didn't wake up until I heard a man yelling bloody murder.

"Hmm?" I said, my eyes still closed.

"So!" he shouted. "Here I've been a good husband for years, worked hard and tried to save, and this happens."

"What happens?" I mumbled, vaguely interested.

"This!"

"Oh," I said. "Huh."

"I thought you were in Los Angeles!" said Jackie.

"Ha!" he said. "I finished my work two days early. I hurry home, and what do I find?"

"What?" I said.

"You!"

"Oh."

"Caught!" said Jackie. "Forgive us, forgive us."

"You!" he said to her. "I'll take care of you, all right."
He turned to me. "You've ruined my home, and now
buster, I'm going to wreck yours. Your wife is going to
hear about this outrage the first thing tomorrow morning. Let's see how you like that!"

"Haven't ruined anything," I said sleepily. "No wife,
either. Wreck away."

"Then I'll wreck your career. See how you like that!"

"Make more money in a defense plant anyway," I said.

There was a lot more yelling that I can't remember,
but it got feebler as time went on, and they finally threw
me out into the hall and locked the door.

***

I slept until noon and didn't get to my office until after
lunch, which I couldn't touch. When I got there, George
was waiting for me.

"Have you got it?" he said.

"The money?" I chuckled, patted him like a father,
and eased him into a chair. "No, George, I haven't. But
I've got news for you. You're off the hook, my boy."

"What hook?" said George. He seemed annoyed.

"George, last night I met a cute little girl named
Jackie. Took her home, in fact."

George turned bright red and stood. "I don't care to
hear about it!"

"Take it easy, take it easy, George. It's the oldest racket in the world, the badger game is, and all you've got to do is to tell 'em to go to hell. They'll back right down. Tell 'em to take your reputation instead of your money, and that's the last you'll ever hear of 'em. Don't give 'em a dime!"

"I don't want to discuss it," said George. "Kindly get me the money this afternoon."

"George," I said, "if you don't stand up to those two, *I'll* go to the cops and press charges. They pulled the same stunt on me. And even if you gave them half of what you've got—that wouldn't be the end, George. You start paying them off, and they won't leave you alone until they get everything—and then some."

"If you have them arrested, we're through," said George.

"If I let you hand over all that money to them, I'll be through with myself," I said. "You've given them a thousand now, and that's a thousand too much."

"I didn't give them a thousand, or anything close to it," said George, "but I plan to. Please get me the money, and keep this matter to yourself. Or must I call a policeman?"

"For them? You bet!"

"For you," said George.

* * *

I was so mad that I walked out on him, and if he'd stood in my way, divinity school or not, I would have knocked him down.

With a clanging headache, I strode around town, piecing together what I knew of the stupid mess George had gotten himself into. Somebody had offered him something he wanted for $519.29, told him to come to the Club Joy to get it; and George, waiting for the seller to show up with the goods, had gotten drunk without meaning to, and had fallen for Jackie and the oldest swindle on earth. QED.

I went to the bank, cashed a check and picked up my statement, and then went into a bar next door for a hair of the dog that bit me—the dog I'd invited to bite me for George's sake.

I leafed through my cancelled checks in the twilight of the bar—nervously and without interest at first, just for something to do. And then I found the check for $519.29, made out by me to George. I turned it over and saw that it was endorsed by George—and by a Robert S. Noonan. I looked up Noonan in the phone directory. He was a private detective.

That's what George had bought, then—a piece of information. That's what had excited him so much, had made him leave his studies and hurry home. That's what he'd been waiting for at the Club Joy, waiting for all evening.

And then I guessed that Noonan hadn't stood up George. Noonan had delivered what he'd been paid for before George had set foot in the Club Joy.

***

Late in the afternoon, I reached George by telephone at the YMCA. "George," I said, "I'm sorry I lost my temper."

"I waited around your office quite a while, hoping you'd come back," said George. "I don't blame you for getting angry. I was very rude."

"I think I understand what it's all about now, George."

"Please," said George, "let's not go through that again. It's a personal matter you couldn't possibly understand."

"George—I guess you've fired me because I didn't get you the money this afternoon. I couldn't, but I'm going to have my little say anyway."

"I don't think you could say anything about the situation that I don't know."

"I can say something that I didn't know until a little while ago. She's your sister, isn't she?"

George was silent for only a moment. "Yes," he said. His voice was dead when he said it.

"Don't get mad at Noonan. He wouldn't tell me a thing. I guessed it myself. Does she know who you are?"

"No. I went to that place just to look at her. I was going to tell her who I was, but apparently what happened to you happened to me."

"And you paid off?"

"Certainly. I was prepared to spend the money on celebrating our reunion anyway. Now, please—you've been very kind to me—won't you get me the money tomorrow? I'm in a hurry to get back to school."

"Sister or not, George—she's a real lady rat," I said.

"There's a child, and there's hope in that," said George. "I am what I am because good people gave me what no one owed me. The best I can do for her, now, too late, is the same. I intend to do the best. I'll see you tomorrow."

* * *

George actually had to catch a late train back to Chicago. I'd sold off half his kingdom, and we'd mailed the proceeds to Jackie in the form of a bank check she'd never be able to trace.

George and I finished a splendid supper, and the question arose as to how we might most pleasantly kill the time remaining until his train.

There was only one place to go, we agreed—the Club Joy. Our visit was purely ceremonial. We ordered drinks, but neither of us could touch them. We just sat there, looking like killers.

Fifteen minutes before train time, we gathered up our coats and hats from Jackie. She looked at us again the way she'd looked at us when we came in: afraid we would turn her in, and hopeful that we were such idiots that we'd not only keep our mouths shut but come back for more.

"Good-night, Jackie," said George.

"Good-night," she said uneasily.

George dropped a dime into her little plate, into a nest of ones and fives.

"A lousy dime?" said Jackie derisively.

"That's all, sister," said George. "Sin no more."

EPISODE FIVE
MISS SNOW, YOU'RE FIRED

Eddie Wetzel was an engineer in charge of making big insulators in the Ceramics Department of the General Forge and Foundry Company in Ilium, New York. Eddie's office was out in Building 59, where there was always a film of white clay dust all over everything.

Eddie was twenty-six. He had strong feelings about beautiful women. He hated and feared them. He had been married to a beautiful woman once—for six fantastic months. In only six months his bride smashed up his friendships, insulted his superiors, put him $23,000 in debt, and turned his self-respect to cinders. When she left him, she took both cars and the furniture with her. She even took Eddie's watch, cigarette lighter, and cuff links. And then she sued him for divorce on the grounds of mental cruelty. She stuck him for $200 a month in alimony.

So Eddie was a pretty serious person when Arlene Snow was assigned to him as a secretary. She was eighteen, petal-fresh out of Ilium High School—and, one month after she joined the company, she was voted the most beautiful girl within the company's seventeen gates. She was voted that on ballots from the company's weekly newspaper, the *GF&F Topics*. Arlene received 27,421 votes out of the 31,623 votes cast.

"You are to be heartily congratulated," Eddie said to her when news of the honor came. "Unfortunately," he said, "our main business here is not sitting around and looking beautiful but manufacturing insulators. So let's get back to work now, shall we?"

He was so sarcastic with her so often that Arlene was delighted whenever an opportunity to get out of the glum and dusty office came along. And the prime opportunity was represented by Armand Flemming, editor of the *GF&F Topics*. Flemming was forty, the brother-in-law of the Vice President in Charge of Employee and Community Relations, the cowed husband of a woman as massive and unyielding as a war memorial. He was constantly borrowing Arlene from the Ceramics Department for use as an unpaid model.

Whenever the company launched a new product, Flemming ran a picture in his paper of Arlene smiling blankly at whatever the new product was. And whenever a holiday was in prospect, Flemming devoted his whole front page to a picture of Arlene that was supposed to express the spirit of the holiday. For the Fourth of July, there was a picture of Arlene in a star-spangled bathing suit, lighting a firecracker as big as she was. The caption was "Kapow!"

And when Halloween came around, there was Arlene being scared out of her little overalls by a jack-o'-lantern. The caption was "Eeeeeek!"

At Thanksgiving time, there was Arlene, dressed like a pilgrim woman from the waist up and like a Las Vegas cigarette girl from the waist down. She was being scared by a turkey, and the caption was "Gobble, gobble, gobble."

It was this last picture that finally caused Flemming's brother-in-law, also his boss, to lower the boom on him. He told poor Flemming that he thought the Thanksgiving picture and its caption were downright dirty. He said, too, that it was obvious to everybody in the company that Flemming was in love with Arlene, since nobody else's picture ever got in the paper anymore, and that Flemming was never to see her again.

As it happened, Arlene was in the offices of the *GF&F Topics* when the riot act was read to Flemming. Fortunately, however, she heard none of it. She was busy in the photography studio, posing in a very scanty Santa Claus suit, with one bare arm draped over the neck of a plaster Rudolph the Red-Nosed Reindeer.

* * *

While Arlene was posing and Flemming was being reamed out, Eddie Wetzel was boiling mad in his office. For want of a secretary, he was typing his own correspondence with two stiff, blunt fingers, and the telephone was ringing incessantly. The calls were never for him, never had anything to do with insulators. The calls were all for Arlene, and all related in one way or another to her unofficial position as company love goddess.

"No—I do not have the slightest idea when she will be back!" Eddie bellowed at a young man on the telephone. "I am merely her supervisor. She never tells me anything." He slammed the telephone into its cradle. He was quite red, and his breathing was shallow and noisy.

Now Arlene and Flemming came in. Flemming was subdued and gray. He hadn't told Arlene what the trouble was. What was bothering him most was his brother-in-law's suggestion that he, Flemming, was in love with Arlene.

Flemming realized, with a breaking heart, that the suggestion was deadly accurate.

Arlene greeted Eddie with the usual uneasiness he made her feel, and then she saw the message he had written in the dust on her desktop. "Miss Snow," he had written in a large round hand, "you're fired."

* * *

Eddie Wetzel made it stick, too. In a manner of speaking, Arlene went right out on her shell-pink ear.

Eddie was able to prove that she was impudent, vain, easily distracted, and a slow and inaccurate typist. She was unable to read her own shorthand, had no loyalty toward the Ceramics Department, held the company record for tardiness and absenteeism, and was as amenable to routines as a one-eyed black cat.

And common sense tempered with cowardice kept anyone else in the company from offering her a job. Any man asking for her services would have raised the question, inevitably, as to just what services he had in mind.

Poor Flemming was least of all free to help her. He slunk back to his office to think things over, and his wife called him up to tell him almost word for word what his brother-in-law had told him, that he wasn't to see Arlene again. She called Arlene *"that hussy."*

When Arlene left the company that evening, there was a pitiful little ceremony at the main gate. She was relieved of her employee's badge—her heavenly face in a clear plastic sandwich. She stood there in the gray and acid slush of winter in Ilium; and the gate guard, complying with company regulations, snipped the badge in two with great tin shears and dropped the halves into an ashcan.

He could not look her in the eye.

Into the night went Arlene, her face simply one more pale pie in a river of pale pies. The sleet-blurred streetlights were not colorful enough to reveal to a passerby that Arlene had been crying.

When she got to her bus stop, Armand Flemming was waiting for her. He was not himself a bus rider. The car he had driven to work was sitting all alone in a company parking lot emptied by the five o'clock rush.

"You riding the bus tonight, Mr. Flemming?" Arlene asked him.

"A bus, an airplane, a train—" said Flemming. "Who knows what I'll be riding before this night is over."

"Pardon me?" said Arlene.

"I'd like to buy you a drink," said Flemming. "I owe you at least that. I feel very responsible for what happened."

"You don't have to," said Arlene.

"I know I don't have to," he said. "I'm tired of doing things I have to do. From now on I'm going to do what I *want* to do." He looked a little wild, but Arlene was too jangled by her own troubles to notice it much. "I insist on buying you a drink."

So Arlene and Flemming went to a quiet little bar down a side street. Its red neon sign winked at them blearily. "Bar," it said. What Arlene and Flemming didn't know was that Eddie Wetzel lived in an apartment over the bar, and that Eddie stopped into the bar every evening for two martinis after work.

Eddie was sitting in his customary booth now, reading a letter from his ex-wife. She still loved him, she said, and could he please send her an extra $142.75? She had had a small accident, she said, and the money would go toward repairing her car. "I don't think it's fair," she wrote, "for me to pay for unexpected things like that, and I'm sure the judge would say the same thing."

The letter was from Miami Beach.

The conversation in the booth next to his now intruded on Eddie's awareness. After a moment of involuntary eavesdropping, Eddie realized who his neighbors were.

"Arlene, I've always followed the line of least resistance," Armand Flemming said. "I've never really taken the bit in my teeth and lived—never done the things I should have done, things I wanted to do."

"That's too bad, Mr. Flemming," said Arlene.

"I haven't pursued happiness," said Flemming.

"I don't guess any of us do, really," said Arlene.

"Then isn't it time?" said Flemming. "Isn't it time we did?" He leaned forward. *"Pendant toute notre vie, Arlene,"* he said, *"jouissons de la vie!"*

"I'm afraid I don't understand that," said Arlene. "I took mostly business courses."

"While we live," said Flemming, covering her hand with his while he translated for her, "let us enjoy life!" Flemming was not fluent in French. He had, in fact, just shot his wad in that particular field. The quotation came from an apron his wife had given him on the previous Father's Day. "Today something in me snapped, and from now on I'm going to *live!*" He cleared his throat. "I want you to live, too!"

"After the things Mr. Wetzel said about me," said Arlene, "I just feel like curling up and dying."

"Forget Eddie Wetzel," said Flemming.

"I don't see how I can," said Arlene. "He's the meanest man I ever knew——" She clouded up. "And for no reason at all. I never did him any harm."

"I'll make you forget him," said Flemming.

"How?" said Arlene.

"By taking you away from all this: sleet, cold, Wetzels, General Forge and Foundry Company, hypocrisy, fear, prudishness, double-dealing, conformity, bullying, compromises, never doing what we really want to do——" said Flemming. "Arlene——" he said, "you are the most beautiful thing that ever came into my life. I can't stand the idea of you going out of it. I love you. I want you to run away with me tonight."

Arlene was shocked. "Mr. Flemming!" she said.

"You know what I did after you were fired?" said Flemming. "I went to my office and thought things over. Then I marched up to the cashier's office, and I demanded my war bonds and I demanded every nickel I'd contributed to the pension fund and I demanded every share of stock I'd accumulated under the stock bonus plan." He opened his suit jacket, showing Arlene that his inner pockets were crammed with negotiable securities. "As I sit here," he said, grabbing her hand, "I am worth $7,419. Where would you like to go, Arlene, to forget Eddie Wetzel and all the twisted, frustrated people like him? Tahiti? Acapulco? The French Riviera? The Vale of Kashmir?"

"Oh, Mr. Flemming—" said Arlene, standing and trying to get her hand back, "I'm very grateful to you, and I appreciate the nice things you've said to me, and I'll always have a special place in my heart for you—but I'd better just go home, I think."

"Home?" said Flemming, standing too, hanging on to her hand. "You think I'd let go of happiness that easily?"

"What makes you so sure I'd *be* your happiness?"

"Haven't you ever looked at yourself?" said Flemming. "Don't you even know what you look like?"

"That was one of the things Mr. Wetzel said—" said Arlene, "that I looked at myself too much."

Flemming knotted his free hand into a fist. "I should have hit him," he said. He showed his teeth. "How I wish I'd hit him!"

"I'm awfully glad you didn't," said Arlene, still trying to get her hand back, get it back without hurting the feelings of the man who wanted to give up everything for her.

"It would have showed you I was a man," said Flemming, full of adrenaline. And then he saw that the opportunity hadn't been lost after all—that Eddie Wetzel was available in the very next booth.

* * *

The fight was brief and unambiguous. Flemming got himself a bloody nose without laying a finger on Eddie Wetzel.

And then the bartender threw Flemming and Eddie and Arlene out of his place, out into the slushy night. "From now on," the bartender said to Arlene, who was already in tears, "do me a favor and bring your boyfriends somewhere else!"

The three went upstairs to Eddie's apartment to make poor Flemming's nose stop bleeding. The apartment, a tiny one, was dismayingly bare. There were no curtains, no rugs, no tables, and only two cheap little kitchen chairs to sit on. The only bed, the narrow bed on which Flemming now lay, was an army-surplus iron cot.

"Oh God—" Flemming said to the ceiling, "no fool like an old fool."

"I didn't mean to hit you that hard," said Eddie. "I'm sorry. I didn't want to hit you at all."

"I wish you'd killed me," said Flemming.

Arlene was in the kitchen, getting ice cubes to pack around Flemming's nose. There was nothing in the refrigerator but one slice of liverwurst and a can of beer. It was a small mystery to her where Eddie ate, since there was no table.

And then she saw the remains of breakfast laid out on top of the refrigerator. That was where Eddie ate, standing up. And there, too, was the only ornamental object in the apartment—the photograph of a bewilderingly beautiful bride in a golden frame.

Eddie came into the kitchen, caught Arlene looking at the picture. "Natalie," he said.

"What?" said Arlene.

"Her name is Natalie," he said. "I guess you know that. All the other girls in the department must have told you about Natalie and me before you'd been working for me a day."

"Yes," she said. "I'm very sorry about what happened to your marriage."

"I was fool enough to think she was as good as she looked," he said. "It was a pretty grim mistake."

"If she was so terrible to you, why do you keep her picture?" she said.

"It's like a man who's been shot wanting the bullet for a souvenir," he said. He dismissed the subject, hurried clumsily on to another one. "Look—" he said, "I'm sorry about what happened today, sorry I had to put you out of a job."

"You explained very well why you had to do it," said Arlene. "It was absolutely fair, I guess. The way you told it, I certainly had it coming."

He worked his hands in the air. "I mean—it isn't really so terrible. It isn't as though you have a family or anything to support."

"That's right," she said. At this point, Arlene would have agreed with him no matter what he said, but her words were as empty as his refrigerator. She was too interested in Eddie as a curious specimen to care much about what she said. She thought she had a good idea now as to what had made his marriage blow up so spectacularly.

"As a matter of fact," said Eddie, "a girl like you probably doesn't even belong in business."

"Where do I belong?" said Arlene watchfully.

Eddie found himself without any reply at all. He was so confused and alarmed by beauty that he could think of no place in the ordinary scheme of things where it could be said to belong.

A long, pitiful moan from poor Flemming put off for a time Eddie having to give Arlene an answer.

* * *

Flemming's nosebleed had stopped of its own accord. Flemming was sitting on the edge of Eddie's jingling cot now, moaning about the mess he had made of his life.

"Things aren't really so awful, are they, Mr. Flemming?" said Arlene. "You can put all the money and bonds and everything back tomorrow."

Flemming shook his head. "The note, the note," he said. As it turned out, he had left a farewell note on his desk, a note that squared everybody off in no uncertain terms, giving the works in particular to his vice-presidential brother-in-law and his battle-ax wife. "The best thing I ever wrote—the only true thing I ever wrote," said Flemming. "I told them I was going to *live*, that I was going to the South Seas and write the great American novel." He shuddered. "They've all read the note by now."

"Then go ahead and do it," said Arlene. "Really go to the South Seas. Really write a book."

"Without you?" said Flemming. Wan hope that she would still run away with him flickered momentarily in his eyes.

"I wouldn't go with you," she said. "I don't love you. I wouldn't do a thing like that."

Flemming nodded. "Of course not," he said. He closed his eyes. "Today was the day I went out of my mind," he said. "Today was the day I went crazy. Today was the day I proved I wasn't a man and ruined my career as a mouse."

"You could still go back to your wife and job—if you want," said Arlene. "Everybody would understand."

"If I want," echoed Flemming. "You, my dear, are all I want."

"You don't even know me," said Arlene. She turned to Eddie. "Neither do you," she said. "I'm just the idea of a pretty girl to both of you. The girl inside of me could change every five minutes, and neither one of you would notice. I think you must have been the same way with your wife," she said to Eddie.

"I was very good to my wife," said Eddie.

"The way you ignore what a woman really is," said Arlene, "a woman has to do all kinds of crazy things just to prove to herself that she's really alive. She'd never find out she was alive from you," she said. "When a girl does something bad," she said, "it's usually on account of somebody isn't paying enough attention to her."

She turned to Flemming. "Thank you for making me so famous," she said. And she left.

* * *

Flemming watched Arlene go, and then he left himself. "It does a man good to get jogged out of his rut from time to time," he said wryly. "Good-night. Sweet dreams."

Eddie assumed that Flemming was going home. And that's where Flemming assumed Flemming was going, too.

But when Flemming, on his way to his lonely car in the middle of the company parking lot, passed Arlene, who was waiting for her bus, Arlene asked him if he was going home.

And he stopped, and he thought it over, and then he said, "Home? Are you nuts?" And he turned around, headed back into town. And he actually did go to Tahiti.

Arlene's bus was slow in coming, so slow that Eddie, who went looking for her, found her before she left his life forever.

"Look—" he said, "could I take you to supper somewhere?"

"Why would you do that?" she said.

"I owe it to you—for everything," he said.

"You don't owe me anything," she said.

"Then I owe it to myself—" he said, "to prove I can treat a nice girl properly." He sighed. "Or is it too late to try and prove that to you now?"

She gave him a small, rueful smile that bespoke a willingness to forgive and forget under certain ideal conditions. "No," she said, "it's never too late for that."

EPISODE SIX
PARIS, FRANCE

Harry Burkhart was the golf pro at the Scantic Hills Country Club in Lexington, Massachusetts. His wife Rachel was an ex-model and a well-known figure skater. When she was in her early twenties she had been offered a part in the Hollywood Ice Review. She married Harry and became a housewife and mother instead. At that time, Harry had become the first football player from the Coast Guard Academy ever to be named All-American by the Associated Press.

When they were both thirty-seven, Harry and Rachel went to Europe for the first time. They went for two weeks—London, Paris, and back home through London again. They couldn't afford a trip even that quick and short. They owed money all over town. But they took the trip anyway, because their doctor and their minister said they had to do something radical and romantic in a game try at not hating each other so.

They had four children to save the marriage for. What the marriage had done for the children so far was to make them the gift of life, and then teach them how to be vain, querulous, and full of hell.

Harry and Rachel had a reasonably good week in London, with plenty of good food and drink, and with money to spend. The money was borrowed, came from the last bit of credit they could possibly get—but there it was, good old money. They always got along better where there was money to spend.

They went by train and boat from London to Paris. When they found their train compartment at Calais, they discovered they were going to share it with two old and demoralized tourists from Indianapolis named Arthur and Marie Futz. The Futzes were in their middle sixties. They, too, were seeing Europe for the first time.

Arthur Futz hated everything he saw. "Europe stinks. England stinks," he said to the Burkharts, as the train began to move. "If I was one of those newsmen over here who broadcast the news home, that's what I'd say every night: 'Europe stinks. This is Arthur Futz, returning you to NBC in New York.'"

Old Futz, a retired plumbing contractor, claimed to have been insulted, cheated, and poisoned in London. "And my God—" he said, "that wasn't even Europe yet." He shook his head. "At least I could understand what they were saying when they gave me the works." He shuddered. "I just wonder," said old Futz, "what new adventures await us in gay Paree."

"We just might have the time of our lives, Arthur," said his wife bleakly. Marie Futz was a sweet, humble, jumpy little thing. She was trying to have a good time, but old Futz wouldn't let her.

"I don't doubt that for a minute," said old Futz. "I bet the French have ways of separating Americans from their traveler's checks as yet undreamed of in other parts of the world."

"It's supposed to be the most beautiful city in the world," said Marie.

"The most beautiful city in the world is Indianapolis, Indiana," said old Futz. "And the most beautiful house in the world is at 4916 Graceland Avenue. And the most beautiful chair in the world is in the living room of that house. And if any money disappears out of my pocket when I'm sitting in that chair, all I have to do is reach in back of the dear old cushion, and there my money is."

"Well—" said Marie emptily, "we'll be back at 4916 Graceland Avenue before we know it." She looked to Rachel Burkhart for sympathy. "And then we'll never budge again," she said. It was so mournful, so full of regret and resignation, the way she talked about never budging again.

"Dumbest thing we ever did was budge in the first place," said old Futz. He pointed to the empty seats in the compartment, seats facing each other by the door. "There's the seats of the two smartest people in the world," he said to Harry and Rachel. "They had brains enough to stay home."

Old Futz now excused himself, went out into the corridor to look for the lavatory. "I just hope I've got enough money to buy myself into the lavatory and back out again, if there is one," he said. "About a hundred dollars each way ought to just about do."

When he was gone, poor Marie Futz couldn't keep herself from shedding a couple of tears. Once Marie'd done that, she told her troubles to the Burkharts. "He's worked so hard all his life that he's never learned how to play," she said. "Play is harder on Arthur than work. This trip was all my idea, and I can see now what a bad idea it was. The minute we got to England, Arthur got all panicky, wanted to call off the rest of the trip, wanted to go back home to 4916 Graceland Avenue."

Marie's next sentence got fainter and fainter. "So I told him, all right, if he really felt that bad, but couldn't we please just go to Paris, France, just for a day, if that's all he could stand it for, but go for a little while, anyway, long enough to see the Eiffel Tower and the *Mona Lisa*, because who knows when we'll ever be so close to Paris, France, again, and who knows how much longer either one of us has to see just a few of the famous, beautiful things outside of the four walls of 4916 Graceland Avenue—?" The end of the question, a whisper, echoed in the bottomless well of human yearning.

"I can see now," said Marie, "how selfish I've been."

"I don't think you've been selfish at all," said Rachel. The miseries of the Futzes were making her feel pretty young still, were making her bloom. Growing old was even tougher on Harry and Rachel than being broke all the time. Coming across really old people had the same soothing effect on them as easy credit.

"People have to grab what they want from time to time," said Harry. He showed off his clever hands, his grabbing hands. Every year those hands lost an appreciable amount of suppleness, but they had a long way to go before they became the tremulous, spotted leaves the hands of old Futz were.

"You can't just spend your whole life doing what other people want you to do," said Rachel. She had a big compact in her hand, as she often did. Palming it, she snapped it open and shut many times in quick succession, made the mirror in it wink and wink at her. What there was to wink at was a thin, athletic brunette who had lost her seeming softness. Her sinews and harsh competitiveness were on the surface now. There was a lot of allure left, but any man attracted was warned at once that Rachel was a plenty tough baby.

Harry and Rachel's momentary feelings of well-being were thin and cheap. How thin and cheap they were was about to be demonstrated. Their feelings of well-being were about to be ripped as easily as wet tissue paper. But even before that ripping took place, Harry and Rachel revealed, in the advice they gave poor Marie Futz, what a rotten couple they made.

"Sometimes people have to go their own way, come hell or high water," said Rachel.

"Sometimes people compromise and compromise until they haven't got any life left," said Harry.

"Life is too short," said Rachel.

And so on. They advised Marie with great amiability, but the things they were saying they had often said to each other, often yelled at each other, with terrible brutality.

Little, white-haired Mrs. Futz was appalled. "I don't mean Arthur and I don't get along," she said. "We'd be lost without each other. I—I shouldn't have said anything. I—I just wish he'd relax and have a nicer time. Nobody's really robbed him or insulted him over here. Everybody's been nice as pie. He just feels lost away from home." She thought awhile, looking for something else to say that would convince the Burkharts that she really had a good marriage. "We love each other very much," she said at last.

"I guess we do, too," said Harry. "I don't know. What the hell. Life's funny."

"I guess we'll make it somehow," said Rachel, her compact winking at her. She liked more and more what the mirror showed.

For Harry and Rachel, this was a moment of high affection. Now Fate, without half-trying, wrecked it. There was an official flurry in the corridor, and a conductor opened the compartment door and pointed out the two unclaimed seats. The boy and girl he pointed them out to were young, luminously good looking, and goofy with love. The boy gave the conductor a tremendous amount of money for his trouble.

And then these two choice children, apparently honeymooners, sat down in facing seats, made each other comfortable with silky touches and misty whispers.

These two found each other so interesting that the others in the compartment could stare at them as much as they liked without giving offense.

Rachel, forced to see what real beauty was, put her winking compact away.

Harry fell in love with the girl immediately, yearned for her shamelessly.

Marie Futz gave an involuntary sigh like a faraway freight whistle.

The boy spoke to the girl in an accent that seemed British. The girl's shy replies were unmistakably Boston Irish. And English wasn't the only language the young man had. He had spoken French liquidly to the conductor.

Arthur Futz returned from the lavatory and was the first to speak to the newcomers. "I walked past here twice," he said. "I saw you two sitting in here, and I figured it was the wrong compartment." He sat down noisily. "'Futz, you old fool,' I said to myself, 'what the heck are you doing lost on a railroad train in France?'"

"It's easy to get lost," said the young man agreeably. He explained that he and the girl had gotten into the wrong compartment, had just been moved to the right one.

"He sure speaks French good," Marie Futz said to her husband. "You should have heard him going with the conductor." She turned to the young man. "That *was* French, wasn't it?" she said.

"Some people have been kind enough to say so," said the young man.

"Arthur and me—" said Marie, "we got French phonograph records and listened to them, only the records talk so slow. You talk so fast, it could be almost any language, as far as I'm concerned. Your wife talks French, too, does she?"

"No," said the young man, "but I'm sure she will."

"I'm sure I won't," said old Futz grumpily.

"There's just one sentence I want to say," said Marie, "and that's 'Take me to the *Mona Lisa* and the Eiffel Tower.'" She turned to Rachel Burkhart, who was looking out the window at the orange roofs and the ranks of poplars. What she was actually seeing was the ghostly reflection of everyone in the dusty windowpane.

And Rachel was burning up.

"You and your husband try those Victrola records?" Marie asked her.

Rachel didn't hear the question. She was watching Harry's reflection in particular, seeing how much Harry pitied himself for not being married to a petal-fresh young dumpling. She clouded up, without showing it, and thought about all the better men she could have had at a smile and a lazy jingle of her bracelet.

Marie Futz, rebuffed by Rachel, put a question to Harry. "You folks know any other languages?"

"German," said Harry. "German is my second language."

Rachel swung her head around to him incredulously. "Whaaaat?" she said.

"Why you always have to pick me up on everything I say?" said Harry, turning the color of tomato juice.

"You can't speak German," said Rachel.

"You don't know everything there is to know about me," said Harry. "I *studied* German at the academy." He didn't mention that he had flunked it as well. He was so lost in a dream of what might have been, what ought to have been, what still might be, that he didn't know what a lie was. He really thought he was bilingual, though he'd never thought so before. Harry suddenly imagined Vienna was his spiritual home, with oceans of beer and waltzing and affectionate, uncritical blond girls bursting their dirndls.

The boy was talking to him now, talking to him in German, inviting Harry to share the pleasures of that barking, growling language.

"I—I didn't quite get all that," said Harry queasily.

The boy said it all again, slowly and distinctly.

Harry considered what had been said to him, and looked as wise as a bullfrog full of buckshot.

Rachel broke the silence with a laugh that sounded like fire tongs being swept through a shelf of champagne glasses. "So typical!" she cried raucously. "How perfectly typical!"

Harry arose slowly, trembling. He stalked out of the compartment, closing the door behind him with a rattle and a bang.

"Well, it *is* typical!" said Rachel, absolutely unrepentant. "He's always imagining he's things he isn't." It took no special crisis to make Rachel sound off about her marriage to strangers. She and Harry had been doing it at the drop of a hat for years. Without knowing it, they had been exploiting the subject as just about the only remotely interesting thing about themselves.

The subject, at any rate, discouraged anybody else from taking the floor for a while. The compartment was reduced to muggy silence.

After a bit, old Futz got out his tickets and his passport, and all the rest of the tossed salad of travel documents. They made him so anxious that others got anxious, too, checked their own documents.

In the conversation that followed, it came out that all three couples would be returning to London in three days. Not only that—they would be sharing the same compartment again.

"I wonder what tales we'll all have to tell," said Marie Futz.

Harry Burkhart never did come back into the compartment. He stayed out in the corridor all the way to Paris, smoking so much that he arrived in the City of Light coughing his head off.

Rachel went out to get him when the train was in the station, claimed him like a cheap suitcase. "Where's your sense of humor?" she asked him.

"Haven't got one," said Harry.

"Paris, honey—Paris, France!" said Marie Futz, full of joy.

"I don't feel good. I don't feel good at all," said old Futz.

The young lovers melted into the Parisian evening at once, blended with it, their coloration perfect, their way made easy by the young man's familiarity with the city and the tongue.

The Futzes and the Burkharts had to find an interpreter to help them claim their baggage, exchange their pounds for francs, and finally tell their cab drivers where they wanted to go.

Waiting at the curb for a cab, Rachel cracked off at Harry again. "Too bad this isn't Germany," she said. "In Germany you'd be king."

Harry swore, took a short walk to work off some of his rage. This tour took him past a beautiful young girl standing under a lamppost. She spoke to Harry in English. She let him know right away that he looked like a hero to her.

In plain view of Rachel, not thirty feet away from her, that girl promised Harry so much love that only a hero would dare take it on.

***

The three couples were booked at different hotels, but here and there they caught glimpses of each other.

Harry Burkhart, for instance, riding an excursion boat down the Seine with a woman not his wife, saw Marie Futz talking with the help of a phrase book to a baffled painter on the riverbank.

Marie Futz, in turn, spotted the marvelous young lovers arguing bitterly on a bench in the garden of the Tuileries.

Old Arthur Futz and a very hollow-eyed Rachel Burkhart ran into each other in the big American drugstore near the Arc de Triomphe. Old Futz was buying Pepto-Bismol. Rachel was buying hair dye and what looked like a half gallon of Chanel No. 5. They didn't speak to each other. Old Futz's fingernails were black, incidentally, and he was a man in a hurry, a man with plenty to do.

Old Futz, moreover, addressed the pharmacist in French. It was stubborn, twanging, billy-goat French, but it was firm and unashamed. The message got through.

And when the three-day visit was over, old Futz got himself and Marie through the Gare du Nord and on board the right train and in the right compartment without the help of an interpreter. He and Marie were the first ones in the compartment, and Marie was gaga over him.

"You got so much more out of those Victrola records than I thought you did," she said, talking about the records from which they'd tried to learn French.

"Didn't learn a damn thing from those records," said Futz. "Any language is just noises people make with their mouths. Somebody makes a noise at me, and I make a noise back at him."

"Nobody understood the noises I made the whole time," said Marie.

"That's because you weren't really talking about anything," said Futz.

Marie accepted this insult meekly. She had wasted the time of an awful lot of Frenchmen with sweet, outgoing, hopeful gibberish.

The next person on board was the lovely young girl—the lovely young girl alone. If love had isolated her from her fellow passengers on the trip to Paris, something a lot less cheerful was doing it now. She didn't greet the Futzes. She took her seat gravely, all thoughts turned inward. She wore no makeup this trip, cloaked herself in the dignity of the intelligent and drab.

She had a watch, but she didn't look at it. She didn't look expectantly into the corridor or out the window. She wasn't waiting for anyone to join her.

The last arrivals were Harry and Rachel Burkhart. There were a policeman, a railroad conductor, a porter, and a young man from the American Embassy with them.

Harry was drunk and disorderly, his tie awry, buttons off his coat, big stains on his elbows and knees. He had a fat lip and a shiner all the colors of fruitcake.

Rachel looked like a white queen of the cannibals. She had bleached her black hair and dyed it Zulu orange. She was cold sober. With a tenderness made all the more touching by her wild appearance, Rachel helped pour Harry on board.

Harry didn't want her tenderness, and he needed it desperately. He alternated between thanking her and telling her to go to hell. Once, when he thanked her, he called her Mother.

When the train began to move, Harry waved to the city and said, "So long, Paris, so long you old—" And he called Paris what the woman he'd spent three days with had been.

The lovely, lonely girl showed flickering interest in this scurrilous farewell, withdrew into herself again.

It took somebody as crazy as Harry to put a blunt question to her. "You can see what happened to *her* husband," he said to the girl, jerking a thumb at Rachel. "So what happened to yours?"

"He's been detained," she said politely.

"Paris sure didn't detain me," said Harry. "I'm one of the most undetained people who ever visited the place." He now stared with glassy speculation at old Futz, rocked back and forth and stared as the train threaded its way between back porches, airing bedding, and enchanted forests of chimney pots. "Mr. Futz—" said Harry.

"Yes?" said old Futz.

"Could I talk to you in private?" said Harry.

"What you going to do now, Harry?" said Rachel uneasily.

"Gonna start running my life again, are you?" said Harry.

"No," said Rachel. She didn't say another word to him.

Harry coaxed a very reluctant old Futz out into the corridor with him.

"I apologize for my husband," said Rachel.

"That's all right," said Marie Futz. "I don't mind. All men do nutty things sometimes."

"Just men?" said Rachel. "Look at my hair."

"Look at my hand," said Marie. She stripped the white glove from her left hand, held it up.

"What about it?" said Rachel.

"No wedding ring," said Marie. "Battered, used old thing—" that old lady said of her wedding ring, "worm almost as thin as a piece of paper in one place." She widened her eyes wonderingly. "Somewhere in that Seine River now, I guess. And when we get back to Indianapolis, Arthur and I'll have to go into some jewelry store, and he'll have to buy a brand new ring for his sixty-five-year-old bride."

The symbolism of a lost wedding ring was so poignant that the lovely girl was caught up in the story. "You lost it off a bridge?" she said.

"Down the drain of a washbasin in the Louvre," said Marie. "Arthur and I had just seen the *Mona Lisa*. Arthur let out a big burp while we looked at that wonderful picture. Then he said there was a good reproduction of it in the Circle Theater in Indianapolis. Then he said he's seen *Saturday Evening Post* covers that made it look sick. Then he said he bet that funny smile on her face was on account of she had heartburn, too.

"So—" said Marie, "I went into the ladies' room, and I cried and cried and cried. He'd squashed my happiness the way he'd squash a cockroach. Without thinking what I was doing, I was taking off and putting on my wedding ring again and again. And then I heard this tinkle, saw that poor old ring go down the drain."

"There wasn't any way of getting it back?" said Rachel, unconsciously treasuring her own wedding ring and ring finger in a hot, tight fist.

"Arthur worked side by side with the French plumbers for three days," said Marie. "Expense was no object. When the plumbers at the Louvre wanted to give up, Arthur put up the money to keep on going. He explored Paris below street level, and I explored it above, and I don't see how either one of us could have had a nicer time. He came up out of the manhole talking French like a native.

"And last night," said Marie, "all the friends he'd made down below threw a party for us. They gave him a crown and me a necklace out of pipe fittings, and they made us King and Queen of the Sewers of Paris."

The train was in open countryside now.

"Considering who we are and what we are and what we've always been," said old Marie Futz, "I can't think of a nicer honor toward the close of life. I'm satisfied now to go back to 4916 Graceland Avenue and never budge again."

The train passed the ruins of a factory that had been bombed in the Second World War.

Orange-haired Rachel looked out at those unsalvageable ruins and said, "I guess Paris gives everybody what he or she's got coming to him or her."

Again the lovely girl was made to turn her thoughts outward. "Wouldn't any city that wasn't your hometown do that?" she said.

"I never saw a city before," said Rachel, "that let a person be so many things so easily. There ought to be a big sign in all the Paris railroad stations, in all the languages, saying, '*This is all a dream. Go ahead and be the fool you are, and see what happens.*'" Rachel touched her hair. "Any minute now, I'll wake up, and my hair will turn back to black again."

"I think it looks very attractive the way it is," said Marie Futz charitably.

"Attractive?" said Rachel with clanking irony. "I'll tell you how attractive it is. I'll tell you how attractive Harry and I both are.

"In Paris, France—" said Rachel, "Harry and I went our own separate ways, lived out our own separate dreams. His way was with a pretty little tart who gave him all the love I'd never given him. She took him for five hundred dollars, his wristwatch, and his cuff links. When his money was gone, she called in her boyfriend, who beat him to a pulp.

"My way," said Rachel, "was to prove how attractive I still was. It didn't take me long to find out. I spent most of the three days hiding in my hotel room, hiding from the kinds of people I attracted: bellhops and drunks over sixty."

The train slowed for a station, but did not stop. It crept past a brick wall on which was chalked in letters six feet high, "Yankee, Go Home."

Rachel and Marie now waited for the girl to tell her story. She never did tell it, to them or to anybody. She didn't long to tell it, because she didn't know if it was something to be proud of or ashamed of or what.

If she had told it, she would have borne out what Rachel said about Paris. And she would have established a deeper tie with Marie Futz, for her story had to do with a wedding ring, too. Her name was Helen Donovan. Though she wore a wedding ring for all to see, Helen was not married, had never been married.

She was a new assistant librarian at the American Embassy in London, the air of Boston still in her lungs. She had been overseas for exactly six weeks—long enough to fall in love with the young man, whose name was Ted Asher—in love enough, far from home enough, to agree to go to Paris with him.

And the only way she got nerve enough to make such an expedition was to buy a wedding ring, to wear it for all to see. Her own fool's dream in Paris had been of holy matrimony. The boy's dream had been of fleeting, easy, carefree love.

The two had scared the daylights out of each other, had parted with Helen's virtue still intact.

Old Futz came back into the compartment. Harry had borrowed money from him, had gone into the dining car for black coffee. "He'll be all right," said old Futz. "He's pretty near sober now."

"What did he say about me?" said Rachel.

"He said he didn't see how a wonderful woman like you ever put up with a bum like him," said Futz.

Rachel went to the dining car to see Harry. The car wasn't really open for business yet. It had just opened to take care of Harry's special emergency. Rachel got in only after explaining that she was a key part of Harry's emergency.

Old Futz was right. Harry was close to sober.

"Hi," said Rachel, sitting down across the table from him.

"Hi," said Harry.

"It's only me," said Rachel.

"Well—" said Harry, "I could certainly make do, if you could."

Rachel answered him by taking his hand.

"I've been sitting here, thinking the craziest things," said Harry. He closed his eyes and pinched the bridge of his nose.

"Like what?" said Rachel.

"Who knows—someday we might even fall in love," said Harry.

"I sure don't love me much anymore," said Rachel.

"Me and myself just had a big bust-up, too," said Harry. "I don't think they'll ever speak to each other again."

"Maybe we could catch each other on the rebound," said Rachel.

And they did catch each other on the rebound. They were like honeymooners on the boat from Calais to Dover—pretty ratty-looking honeymooners, but honeymooners all the same.

On another part of the boat, Marie Futz unwrapped a plaster model of the Eiffel Tower two feet high. It was a surprise present for her husband. It had a barometer in it, made in Japan, and old Futz discovered right away that the barometer was permanently stuck at *ouragan*.

"It's the thought that counts," said old Futz. "Thank you very much."

Back in the stern of the boat, young Helen Donovan stood all alone, hypnotized by the wake. She took off her spurious wedding ring and threw it at France.

A Frenchman standing nearby saw her do it. He went up to her and said, "Pardon, Madame—I could not 'elp viewing zee dramatic zing you do."

His name was Gaston DuPont, a Renault salesman. Gaston was on his way to raise hell in what he considered the most immoral city in the world, London. He thought he was making a whale of a beginning, finding a good-looking girl who had just thrown away her wedding ring.

Gaston was wrong. Helen rejected his guardedly indecent proposals.

Poor Gaston, spurned by Helen, fell in with evil companions when he got to London. He was royally rooked by many people but in particular by a Piccadilly tart name Iris. After three days in London, Gaston looked worse than Harry Burkhart had after three days in Paris.

Helen Donovan started to write a novel about *her* three days in Paris. But the first two lines she wrote put her right out of the novel business again.

"Love is a funny thing," she wrote. "I don't think I'm old enough yet to understand everything there is to know about it."

EPISODE SEVEN
THE LAST TASMANIAN

A Nonfiction Essay, Sagaponack, 1992

Why did it go on for so long? I look at maps, and I simply can't believe that it went on for so long. I am speaking of the *non-discovery of America* by Europeans. It went on until 1492! That is practically only the day before yesterday! I ask you: Who *couldn't* have found half of a planet as small and navigable as this one is?

Daredevils have since crossed the Atlantic in rowboats and sailboats no bigger than a sofa, and have been rewarded with yawns and minor mentions in *The Guinness Book of Records*. I think of Europeans before 1492, and I am reminded of my regimental commander during World War II, in which I served as a foot soldier. We used to say of him that he couldn't find his own behind while using both hands.

* * *

About twenty years ago I wrote an essay that was printed by the *New York Times* about how inhospitable the moons and asteroids and other planets in the solar system were, so that we would be wise to quit treating this planet as though, in case we wrecked it, there were plenty of spares out there. Letters from readers poured in, most of them saying that I was the sort of person who would have told Christopher Columbus to stay home. They honestly believed, as nearly as I could tell, that, if it weren't for Columbus, we Europeans still wouldn't know about the Western Hemisphere, and General Motors wouldn't now be laying off seventy thousand workers, and Los Angeles wouldn't be running out of water, and we wouldn't have killed a high-school teacher while trying to put her into orbit, and so on.

* * *

The great graphic artist Saul Steinberg, a native of Romania, now a resident of New York City, thanks to Christopher Columbus and Adolf Hitler, told me once that he could not commit political history to memory—when Caesar lived, when Napoleon lived, and so on—until he related it to what artists were doing at such and such a time. Art history was what he was born to care about. He made art history a spine to which to attach whatever else might have been going on.

My big brother, the physical chemist Dr. Bernard Vonnegut, who studies the electrification of thunderstorms, gives his view of history a spine of scientific insights—Newton's laws of motion and Einstein's $E=mc^2$ and so on—to which he attaches kings and generals and politicians and explorers and so on. I myself, as a writer, make a spine of works of literature. But most United States citizens, without such specialized enthusiasms, have been given by their teachers a spine of dates to memorize, most prominent among them 1066, when the Normans invaded England, since we all get English history and attitudes along with the language; and 1492, without which we wouldn't exist; and 1776, when we became a beacon of liberty to the rest of the world, slavery and all; and 1941, December 7, to be exact, when the Japanese, without warning, sank a lot of our fleet at Pearl Harbor in the Hawaiian Islands, on, as Franklin Delano Roosevelt said, "a date which will live in infamy."

But making a spine for history out of memorized dates has the side effect of teaching that human destiny is governed by sudden and explosive events, strictly localized in space and time. The truth is that we are the playthings of systems as complex and turbulent as the weather systems pondered by my big brother Bernard. So the reasonable way to think about Columbus and his toy armada, it seems to me, is that he was part of a system of European explorers, a sort of tropical storm that was bound to hit the outlying islands of the Western Hemisphere, the other half of this little planet, after all, in 1492, give or take, say, thirty years.

* * *

We like to pretend that so many important discoveries have been made on a certain day, unexpectedly, by one person rather than by a system seeking such knowledge, I think, because we hope that life is like a lottery, where simply anyone can come up with a winning ticket. Paul of Tarsus, after all, became the leading theologian of Christianity in a flash, while on the road to Damascus, didn't he? Newton, after being hit on the head by an apple, was able to formulate a law of gravity, wasn't he? Darwin, while idly watching finches during a brief stopover on the Galápagos Islands during a voyage around the world, suddenly came up with a theory of evolution, didn't he? Who knows? Tomorrow morning, some absolute nobody, maybe you or I, might fall into an open manhole and return to street level with a concussion and a cancer cure.

Perhaps we are so fond of instant discoveries that I have to say didactically that St. Paul and Newton and Darwin, like Columbus, had long pondered whatever puzzle it was that they eventually solved, or seemed to solve, and that they had plenty of similarly inspired company while trying to solve it.

* * *

I said to a Jewish friend recently, Sidney Offit, a novelist who occasionally comments on political matters on TV, that I had heard from somewhere that Christopher Columbus might have been Jewish.

"Oh God," he exclaimed. "I hope not."

"I meant to delight you," I said truthfully. "Why would you hope not?"

"We're in enough trouble already," he said.

Sydney was acknowledging two stressful subjects at once: the Gentile habit of making scapegoats of Jews, of course; and the growing body of opinion here that the behavior of Columbus and so many of the Europeans who came after him toward the Native Americans, the people who had already discovered America, was loathsome, to say the least. Our mutual friend, the historian and ardent conservationist Kirkpatrick Sale, had just published a generally well-received book, *The Conquest of Paradise*, which proved by means of contemporaneous documents that Columbus, far from being a hero, was almost insanely greedy and cruel.

* * *

Our friend Kirkpatrick concludes in his book that Europeans came ashore "in what they dimly realized was the land of Paradise...but all they ever found was half a world of nature's treasures and nature's people that could be taken, and they took them, never knowing, never learning the true regenerative power there, and that opportunity was lost. Theirs was indeed a conquest of Paradise, but as is inevitable with any war against the world of nature, those who win will have lost—once again lost, and this time perhaps forever."

Wham! All of a sudden Kirkpatrick brings us up to the present day, and how we continue to wreck this place like vandals! The amount of garbage I produce each week is surely a case in point. It is picked up every Tuesday morning in this village with an Indian name on the tip of Long Island. I don't know where they take it. It simply disappears like whatever it was that seemed so important on TV only a few days ago. I am allowed only three cans of garbage a week. Anything more than that I have to get rid of myself somehow, and I already have three full cans of garbage. What to do? The Sunday edition of the *New York Times*, which I will pick up tomorrow morning, is all by itself bulky enough to fill a fourth garbage can.

* * *

Europeans are commonly uncomfortable when I call
myself a German. When I accepted a prize in Sicily
last year, I said that it was most gratefully received by
both an American and a German. Several persons
said afterward that they had not realized that I was
born in Germany, which, actually, was not my case. If
I had been born in Germany instead of Indianapolis,
Indiana, in 1922, I would almost certainly have been
a corpse on the Russian Front. My parents and grand-
parents were also born in Indianapolis, the first community in the United States, incidentally, where a
white man was hanged for the murder of an Indian. It
was my great-grandparents who were the immigrants,
all Germans, literate and middle class, the males farm-
ers and businessmen. They arrived too late to see the
hanging. Better still, they were too late to have anything to do with the enslavement of black Africans or
the extermination of the Indians, horrible achieve-
ments by Anglos and Spaniards and Portuguese, and
here and there by Dutch and French, and, of course,
mercenaries like Columbus.

The worst of the dirty work had been done, so
my ancestors could feel as innocent as Adam and Eve
as they built their homes and founded their schools
and libraries and symphony orchestra, and so on, on
fertile land where nobody had ever lived before, or
so it seemed. And they were fruitful and multiplied,

but continued to think of themselves, as do I, as Germans.

* * *

"Behind every great fortune lies a great crime," said Balzac, alluding to European aristocrats who imagined themselves to be descended from anything other than sociopaths. Count Dracula comes to mind. Yes, and the coinage of every Western Hemisphere nation might well be stamped with Balzac's words, to remind even the most recent arrivals here from the other half of the planet, perhaps Vietnamese, that they are legatees of maniacs like Columbus, who slit the noses of Indians, poked out their eyes, cut off their ears, burned them alive, and so on.

And while I and my children and grandchildren are entitled to say, as aftershocks of old atrocities continue to be felt by Indians and blacks, that our family never killed an Indian or owned a black, we can scarcely opine that Germans are gentler, kinder, saner than other Europeans. Would we dare? Does anybody perchance remember World War II? For those who never heard of it and its gruesome preamble, there are movies they can see. Word of honor, it really happened. All of it.

Yes, and Heinrich Himmler, a German chicken farmer Adolf Hitler put in charge of killing Jews and

Slavs and homosexuals and Jehovah's Witnesses and
Gypsies and so on in industrial quantities, once delivered
a touching speech to his underlings, who were doing the
tormenting and killing day after day, in which he praised
them for sacrificing their humane impulses in order to
achieve a greater good.

* * *

Another native German Heinrich, Heinrich Böll, a great
writer, and I became friends even though we had once
been corporals in opposing armies. I asked him once
what he believed to be the basic flaw in the character of
Germans, and he replied "obedience." When I consider
the ghastly orders obeyed by underlings of Columbus, or
of Aztec priests supervising human sacrifices, or of senile
Chinese bureaucrats wishing to silence unarmed, peaceful protesters in Tiananmen Square only three years ago
as I write, I have to wonder if obedience isn't the basic
flaw in most of humankind.

* * *

And it is Monday now. I mustn't forget: Tuesday in this
part of the New World is Garbage Day.
      When I was in Sicily, accepting a prize for my book
Galápagos, which argued that human beings were such

terrible animals because their brains were too big, every-one was suddenly talking about a story that had just appeared in the papers and on TV. It said that American troops with bulldozers had buried alive thousands of Iraqi soldiers in tunnels where they were hiding from our shells and bombs and rockets. I answered without hesitation that American soldiers could not be found who would do a thing that heartless.

Wrong again.

* * *

The key words in the previous paragraph are "TV" and "bulldozers." These are man-made devices that, like rockets and artillery and war planes, and like the most expensive individual artifacts ever made by *Homo sapiens*, nuclear submarines, do more to comfort chicken-hearted underlings, should they be ordered to commit atrocities, than any inspirational speech by Columbus or Heinrich Himmler. I myself would not have thought of a bulldozer as such an instrument, had I not been trained during World War II to operate the largest tractors then used by our army, not for bulldozing, as it happened, but for dragging siege howitzers (240 mm) over rough terrain. If a blade had been fixed on the front of one, I might have bulldozed just about anything, with only a dim idea of what all was actually happening up front or underneath, as I sat high in the air, atop a lurching, quaking, roaring, clanking, cosmically insensitive juggernaut.

As for TV: I was about to say that it was a leading personality of our time, but now, still the day before Garbage Day, I am moved to declare it the *only* personality of our time, at least in the USA. I suggest that another date our children might be encouraged to memorize along with 1066, 1492, 1776, and 1941, not that they can remember much of anything anymore, thanks to TV, is 1839. That is when the French physicist Alexandre-Edmond Becquerel, according to the *Encyclopaedia Britannica*, "observed that when two electrodes are immersed in a suitable electrolyte and illuminated by a beam of light, an electromotive force is generated between the electrodes." If light could be turned into electricity, and if electricity could be turned into radio waves, and if radio waves could be turned back into electricity, and if electricity could be turned back into light, hey, presto! TV!

* * *

My adopted son Steve Adams wrote funny stuff for TV out in Los Angeles for a while. He made a lot of money, but he had to quit. He could not stand it anymore that every joke he wrote had to refer to something that had been big news on TV during the past two weeks. Otherwise, his audience wouldn't know what he was having fun with. TV was expected to be a great teacher, but its shows are so well done that it has become the only teacher, and an awful teacher, since there is no way for it to make its students learn by doing something. Worst of all, it keeps saying that whatever it has taught in the past doesn't matter anymore, that it has found something much more entertaining for us to look at.

So the wake of North American TV is something like the wake of a bulldozer, in which everything has been made nice and neat, dead level and lifeless and featureless. But a better analogue of TV's wake in the space-time continuum is a black hole into which even the greatest crimes and stupidities, and indeed whole continents, if need be, can be made to disappear from our consciousness.

* * *

I was trained many years ago by the University of Chicago to be an anthropologist, but I could find no work as such because I did not earn a doctorate. I have since inquired as to what became of my classmates who did go on to attain that rank, given that there weren't any primitive people around anymore. I was told that they had become "urban anthropologists." The slums of the richest nation on Earth are now their deserts, their ice caps, their jungles dark, where everybody but the urban anthropologists, thanks to the Second Amendment of the Constitution of the United States of America, seems to have a firearm. Bullets are flying everywhere.

The Second Amendment, written by the Anglo James Madison, a slave owner, says, "A well-regulated Militia, being necessary to the security of a free State, the right of the people to keep and bear Arms, shall not be infringed." As long as the poor people in this country kill each other, which is what so many of them are doing day after day, the federal government, obviously, is content to regard them, as Columbus might have done, as a well-regulated militia.

* * *

And, oh my gosh, I almost forgot! It's Tuesday morning! Today is Garbage Day! I will have to stand on top of the contents of a full-to-the-brim garbage can and jump up and down until I have made room for the Sunday *Times*.

OK, I have done that now. A big problem with garbage out here, aside from where the garbage men are supposed to put it after they have collected it, is created by raccoons (*Procyon lotor*) and opossums (*Didelphis virginiana*), both mammals that are omnivorous, nocturnal, and unbelievably cunning at getting the lids off garbage cans. I have heard that the North and South American continents were once separated by water, long before

Columbus got here, long before any sort of human being got here. When a land bridge finally married the two land masses, we got some of their unique animals, and they got some of ours. They got our raccoons and we got their opossums, the only marsupials in the whole New World, incidentally, the worst possible news for garbage cans from Tierra del Fuego to Hudson Bay.

* * *

If I were worth my salt as an anthropologist, which I am not and never was, I would be writing now about the intermingling of Christianity and Native American religions instead of opossums and raccoons. But whatever it was that Columbus and so many of the Europeans who encountered Native Americans after him thought they were practicing, couldn't have been inspired by the Christian masterpiece, the Sermon on the Mount.

Kirkpatrick Sale tells of Taino Indians who buried Christian icons in their fields in order to increase the fields' fertility. This was a reverent thing for them to do, but Columbus's brother Bartolomé had the Indians burned alive. On several occasions the Spaniards hanged thirteen Indians at once, with their feet barely touching the ground, in honor of Jesus and the twelve Apostles. And of course the Christian Adolf Hitler back in the Old World, not that long ago, had the men who had conspired to assassinate him hanged from meat hooks by piano wire, with their feet barely touching the ground, and had their comical jigs of death filmed by a professional camera crew.

* * *

Let us give poor old Columbus a rest. He was a human being of his times, and aren't we all? We are all so often bad news for somebody else. AIDS, I read somewhere, was probably brought into this country by a Canadian flight attendant on an international flight. And what had his crime been? Nothing but love, love, love. That's life sometimes. And he is surely as dead as Columbus now. And I'm killing the world with garbage, three cans a week, sort of like Chinese water torture.

Speaking of Chinese tortures: I saw a wood engraving one time of a Chinese woman who had been tied down, and some Chinese men were encouraging a Chinese stallion to copulate with her, which, as a caption explained, would kill her. She must have done something wrong, or this wouldn't have been done to her. Not in so many words, certainly, but she must have asked for it.

And then there was the Christian Croatian Nazi in my time, although I was a mere youth then, who kept a bowl of human eyes on his desk. It was common for visitors to at first mistake them for hard-boiled eggs.

* * *

Tempus fugit! It is the day-after-Garbage Day! My three cans are again as vacant and inviting as was Indiana when my immigrant ancestors, without opposition, picked out their homesites there. I can again give my full attention to my cat Claude, a sensuous white male with one blue eye and one yellow eye, speaking of eyes. There are only the two of us here, in a house which appears on a map drawn in 1740. I have calculated that Claude's and my house is twice as old as the theory that invisible germs can cause disease. A woman who knows a lot about cats, or pretends to, told me that white cats with eyes like Claude's are deaf on the side of the blue eye.

I have yet to devise an experiment that can confirm this, or, alternatively, to demonstrate that the woman is as full of shit as a Christmas turkey. I am sixty-nine years old now, and my father didn't go to the New World in the sky until he was seventy-two, so I still have lots of time in which to experiment on Claude. I will need some apparatus, and there will be a temporary loss of dignity on the part of Claude. But without experimentation on lower animals, this world would be an even worse place than it is today. And Claude tortures mice before he kills

them. Like Christopher Columbus, he knows nothing of
the Beatitudes.

***

This part of Long Island has become a summer resort
for some of the wealthiest human beings in history so
far, many of them Europeans, particularly Germans. It
is known generically as "the Hamptons." The political
unit of which Claude and I are part is Southampton, but
our village, again, an Indian name, is Sagaponack.

I am out here in the wintertime, with all the rich
people generating garbage in Palm Beach and Monte
Carlo and so on, because of certain problems with my
marriage, which my wife and I hope are only temporary.
I think she is Columbus and I am the Indians, and she
thinks I am Columbus and she is the Indians. But we are
calming down.

***

And now is as good a time as any to review my own
relationship with what is left of the real Indians, or, as
they prefer to be called, Native Americans. One time my
wife and I invited a man who we thought was a Native
American to the Russian Tea Room, an expensive restaurant in Manhattan, on Thanksgiving Day, the most

agreeable of all our national holidays. It commemorates a feast in 1621 given by English invaders of what is now Plymouth, Massachusetts, to which Native Americans came as most welcome guests.

Our guest, while born in New York City, was customarily dressed in bits of costumes of many tribes, Navajo jewelry, Iroquois fringed deerskin, Cree moccasins, and so on, and was much respected as a speaker and writer on Native American affairs, and the writer of excellent novels about who he claimed were his people. He never wore a necktie, and the Russian Tea Room at that time had a rule, since honored in the breach to a fare-thee-well, that all male patrons had to wear ties.

I telephoned the restaurant and received in advance a suspension of the rule, in view of our guest's proud and respectable ethnicity. As I recall, we had blintzes with salmon caviar and sour cream, washed down with Stolichnaya vodka. That was about it. It was nice. But then, a couple of years later, several tribes of indigenes protested that this man, while he had served their cause nobly, was a white man pretending to be a Native American. Who knows? The last time I saw him, he was dressed like a Wall Street broker, but with one turquoise earring, which, since the stone's setting was of fine silver wires, I took to be the handiwork of

Zunis, stubbornly superstitious aborigines in faraway New Mexico.

* * *

Other contacts I have had with Native Americans haven't been that ambiguous. When I was a youth I spent two summers roaming with friends through Arizona and Colorado and New Mexico, observing if not befriending Hopis and Navajos, and, yes, Zunis. We were fortunate enough to hear some of their songs and see some of their dances, and to have the opportunity to buy their artifacts without having to pay extra to an intervening white entrepreneur or two. But I must say that those people had my sympathy and admiration long before I got close enough to one to touch them and their kids.

Even when I was in the first grade in school in Indianapolis, where there were no Indians, or so few that I never heard about them, I think I knew that Indians were innocent victims of crimes by white men that could never be forgiven by me, by anyone. Almost all of my schoolmates felt the same way, and our teachers did, too. It was so obvious, once we learned that Indians used to have their homes where we lived. If we kept a sharp lookout when we walked through woods or along riverbanks, we could actually find their arrowheads. I myself used to have a collection of maybe twenty or more of those. Why would anybody have departed voluntarily from a region so salubrious?

* * *

As a lifelong Indian lover, I am shocked when I meet white people who live near a lot of Indians and have nothing but contempt for them. They are not numerous, and in my experience have almost all been members of our overtly white-supremacist and social-Darwinist political party, the party of Presidents Ronald Reagan and George Bush, the Republicans.

There is much worse to report: I have read about, but never seen, out-of-print writings by my particular literary hero, Mark Twain, in which he speaks of Indians, of whom he had seen plenty, as though they were subhuman, almost vermin. So again, who knows? Maybe they are like that Chinese woman who was tied down and killed by the penis of a stallion. Whatever the Native Americans got and are still getting, maybe they asked for it.

* * *

I correspond regularly with a Sioux named Leonard Peltier, who is serving two consecutive life sentences with no hope of parole, in the federal prison at Leavenworth,

Kansas. He has become famous since it has become ever clearer that he was wrongly convicted for the fatal shooting of one or both agents of the Federal Bureau of Investigation killed on Indian property near Oglala, South Dakota, during a confused shootout in 1975. An Indian was also killed, and there can be no doubt that Indians did some shooting.

My friend Peter Matthiessen, who lives half a mile from here, wrote a book about the incident and its aftermath, *In the Spirit of Crazy Horse*. In it he declares, "The ruthless persecution of Leonard Peltier had less to do with his own actions than with underlying issues of history, racism, and economics, in particular Indian sovereignty claims and growing opposition to massive energy development on treaty lands and the dwindling reservations." In any case, evidence has now been uncovered, including a confession by the man who really did the killing, that Peltier didn't deserve even one life sentence, not even a minor fraction thereof.

Several months ago, it may have been on what was Garbage Day out here, this new evidence was brought to the attention of a federal judge in a petition that Peltier be given a new trial. The judge's decision is pending, but what a prosecutor said was noteworthy for its pigheadedness. He said, in effect, and I don't have his exact words, that if Peltier wasn't guilty of murder, he was sure as heck guilty of something almost as bad. [Editor's note: That petition, and all subsequent actions, have been denied. Peltier remains in prison.]

This rang a bell with me. I had written some about the Italian-American anarchists Nicola Sacco and Bartolomeo Vanzetti, who were electrocuted in Massachusetts for the murder of a payroll guard, in 1927, when I was only five. I knew that one of their prosecutors had said very much the same thing about them, that they were certainly guilty of something terrible, although unspecifiable in court. Again, another man had confessed to the crime, but they went to the "hot seat" anyway. Vanzetti sat down in the chair before he was told it was time to do so, just as though he were in his own living room. I told Peltier in a letter about the similarities between their prosecutors and his, and added what I think is true: The Italians back in the 1920s and earlier seemed as non-white to this country's ruling class as Indians. And so seemed Greeks and Jews and Spaniards and Portuguese.

* * *

In a P.S. to the letter I said that Al Capone, the Chicago gangster, was asked if his fellow Italian immigrants should be executed, and he replied, "Yes." When asked why Massachusetts should kill them, Capone said, "They are ungrateful to this wonderful country." That could be true of Leonard Peltier as well. His last name is pronounced "Pelter." The capital of his native state, Pierre, South Dakota, is pronounced "Peer." Very little French is spoken there. Al Capone was sent to prison for not paying income tax.

***

I apologize for writing as though the United States were the entire Western Hemisphere, and as though Claude were the only cat here, half-deaf or otherwise. But the first rule taught in any creative-writing course, and I think it's a good one, is: "Write what you know about."

***

Robert Hughes, an Australian who has become this nation's most intelligent art critic and a historian of his native land as well, has written disapprovingly in *Time* magazine of Kirkpatrick Sale's *The Conquest of Paradise*. He says that, while the heroism of Columbus was a myth pleasing to white supremacists, Sale served the truth no better by making Columbus "like Hitler in a caravel, landing like a virus among the innocent people of the New World."

The smallest state in Hughes's Australia, the island of Tasmania, is the only place on Earth where the entire native population was dead soon after the first white people arrived, and whose genes are no longer to be found even in crossbreeds, since the settlers found Tasmanians so loathsome that they would not have sex with them. It is not certain that the Tasmanians had even domesticated fire.

At the University of Chicago so long ago, one professor suggested to me that the Tasmanians found life so intolerable after the white people came that they stopped having sex with each other.

Contrast, if you will, all that celibacy in the Tasman Sea with this uninhibited frolic in 1493, in the Caribbean: "While I was in the boat I captured a very beautiful Carib woman, whom the said Lord Admiral gave to me...I conceived desire to take pleasure...but she did not want it and treated me with her fingernails in such a manner that I wished I had never begun. But...I took a rope and thrashed her well, for which she raised such unheard of screams that you would not have believed your ears. Finally we came to an agreement in such a manner that I can tell you that she seemed to have been brought up in a school of harlots."

That is an account by an Italian nobleman, and I have lifted it from Sale's book. The Lord Admiral, of course, was Columbus. And one is surely not reminded of Hitler, whom Sale mentions nowhere, since Hitler was virtually as celibate as the last Tasmanian, sexually beyond reproach.

***

During the Second World War it was generally believed by Hitler's enemies that he had only one testicle. I confess that I believed it. We will never know, I suppose, who started that rumor. But Russians who took possession of Hitler's charred remains in Berlin counted his testicles, and he had two of them. It is also not true that the Nazis made soap and candles of fat rendered from the corpses of concentration-camp victims. I myself helped to spread that story in a novel, *Mother Night*, and have received enough letters from dispassionate fact-gatherers to persuade me that I had been misleading. Mea culpa.

I once worked for a man who was so stupid he believed that all women menstruated on the same day of the month, that they were all controlled by the moon. I certainly never passed *that* on.

***

What I have seen with my own two eyes, though, and can easily see again whenever I please, is a nuclear submarine, under construction or slumbering on the surface of the Thames River at Groton, Connecticut. Several of these things operating in concert, and we have several of them, are capable of killing everybody in the other hemisphere, as though there were dozens of hemispheres instead of only two. Yes, and the Soviet Union, which has had the grace to vote itself out of existence, had the same sort of high-tech, whiz-bang, guilt-free, hemisphere-killing, undersea leviathans. I can't help thinking that it is somehow symbolically significant that, on the five hundredth anniversary of the end of Europe's non-discovery of America, each hemisphere had thought it might become necessary to kill the other one, but had suddenly changed its mind about that.

On this side of the water at least, TV, our great teacher, our endlessly diverting teacher, our only teacher, has had a lot to do with this change of heart, as well as with the elaborate preparations for suicide that preceded it. It has made all our enemies vanish into the black hole in its wake. It is as though they never existed. Until practically the day before yesterday, we were loved by only some countries. Now all countries love us, and we should feel like Marilyn Monroe standing over an air vent in the sidewalk, with her skirt blowing up around her ears, absolutely adorable!

* * *

If it weren't for TV, we might now be, to use one of our many colorful expressions, "standing around with egg on our face," since we are stuck with all this doomsday apparatus that has no sane purpose, and that sopped up so much of our wealth that our bridges and schools and hospitals and so forth are falling down.

To "stand around with egg on one's face," as nearly as I can explain it to somebody who doesn't actually live here, is to display charming embarrassment or perhaps winsome silliness about one's participation in an enterprise that was supposed to be necessary, logical, and all-round wonderful, but that turned out to be the exact opposite. But TV is making the weapons disappear by having us look elsewhere.

To "stand around with egg on one's face" is not to be confused with "standing around with one's thumb up one's fundament," which means not knowing what to do next, as does "not knowing whether to defecate or wind one's watch."

* * *

Robert Hughes's disparagement of my friend Kirkpatrick Sale's book is but a tiny part of a long polemic by him against all who depict European colonists as having been purely evil, and the natives they distressed as having been purely virtuous. But Hughes or anyone else reading Sale's documented account of what Columbus and his men did and what the Tainos and Caribs did upon finding themselves intermingled would be hard put to say what persons of a philosophical turn of mind like to say whenever possible: "There was blame enough for everyone."

Nor does Hughes imply as much. What really bothers him, as near as I can tell, is that historians like Sale, although truthful, encourage large numbers of foolish people of all races to believe that persons of European descent in this hemisphere right now still represent pure evil, and that the descendants of the hideously abused Indians and black slaves are charmingly innocent, or would have been, if only white people had never troubled them.

Sale himself is not that foolish. What he does say in one way or another is that white people over here still hold most of the power, and continue to be slovenly and greedy custodians of an ecological system that might still, with a good deal of effort, become something approaching Paradise.

* * *

Robert Hughes's employer, *Time* magazine, has been publishing once a week since 1923, when I was only one year old. Within my own memory, I can't recall a single issue in which *Time* appeared to be standing around with egg on its face or with its thumb up its fundament. Others could be mistaken, but never *Time*. Its founder,

Henry Robinson Luce (1898–1967), declared this to be "The American Century," "America" to him and his readers being the United States. And *Time* continues to be profoundly sympathetic with those at the top of the white power structure here, no matter what a bad job they may be doing, on the grounds, I suppose, that it isn't easy to be on top. But the writers and editors of *Time* today are unlikely to feel in their personal lives the aplomb of their magazine. The enormous corporation of which they are mere particles has gone into debt on a catastrophic scale, in order to enrich a very few of its top executives. It does not appear to have revenues adequate to pay even the interest on its debts.

Several employees of *Time* have been laid off as economy measures, and those remaining are entitled to feel as the Tainos and Caribs should have felt in 1492, when the first Europeans beached their longboat, stepped out on the sand with their firearms and edged weapons at the ready, and began to look around.

I do not mean that those laid off or about to be laid off by *Time* can expect to be enslaved or hanged in batches of thirteen or whatever. But they will surely experience severe acculturation, as will the seventy thousand workers recently laid off by General Motors, and many will feel as lonesome and unwanted on Earth, until they find new jobs, God willing, as did, surely, the last Tasmanian. They, and all the others in Henry Robinson Luce's

America who are facing unemployment, are as blameless and powerless as persons caught in an avalanche.

* * *

And when I think of avalanches, or indeed of tremendous, unopposable forces of any sort, I am reminded of an English friend of my big brother and me, John Latham, an atmospheric scientist like my brother, but a poet and humorist as well. He has been working for years on a book of advice for travelers in foreign lands, and one of his chapters tells how you should behave after being hit by an avalanche, in the Himalayas, say. The first rule is do not panic. The second rule is, after you have been buried alive, and all movement of rocks and snow around you has stopped, find out which way is up. John says, as I recall, that this can be done by dangling a pocket watch or a locket at the end of its chain. Yes, and much useful information can be garnered, he says, if you study the behavior of snow fleas that may have been buried with you.

Mark Twain, not long before he died a bitter old man, was writing a book much like John Latham's, pretending to be helpful but actually calling attention to how humbling life, and especially its endings, can be. Twain's was about etiquette. His advice on how to behave at a funeral, I remember, included, "Do not bring your dog." Like Latham, he chose to laugh in agony rather than sob in agony about how irresistible forces, whether physical or economic or biological or political or social or military or historical or technological, can at any time smash our hopes for moderately happy and healthy lives for ourselves and our loved ones to smithereens.

* * *

Robert Hughes and many others like him may dislike histories like *The Conquest of Paradise* because they are tearjerkers, making us sympathize with the miseries of nobodies long gone, like the Carib beauty who was whipped and whipped, or like the last Tasmanian, also a woman, rather than celebrating the grandeur of history when viewed from afar. But when I ask myself now of what that grandeur could possibly consist, I can come up with only one answer: The millions and millions of us who, in spite of all the atrocities, are still OK.

* * *

My first wife, née Jane Marie Cox, now dead of cancer, was such an adept student of literature in college that she was nominated by the English Department for the highest honor, which was election to Phi Beta Kappa, a national society of our most diligent students. Her election was opposed by the History Department, whose wares she had denounced often and vocally as being as void of decency as child pornography. She was in good company of course, as I am able to demonstrate with the help of Bartlett's *Familiar Quotations*: "History is but the record of crimes and misfortunes," Voltaire; "History is a nightmare from which I am trying to awake," James Joyce; and on and on. Jane's champions pointed this out to her enemies, and they prevailed. She became a Phi Beta Kappa.

I knew Jane back then, when she was the focal point of that controversy, and thought her stubborn stand attractive but wrongheaded. Back then, I still believed, as I do not believe nowadays, that the human condition was improving despite such heavy casualties. We are incorrigibly the nastiest of all animals, as our history attests, and that is that.

* * *

I have said almost nothing about those of us in the USA who are the descendants of black African slaves. Well over half of them, as any fool can see, are also variously English or Scottish or Irish or Native Americans. The fact that so many of them are white as well as black is as seldom mentioned in polite conversations by whites as the fact that the crosses on the Nazis' tanks and planes testified that those inside believed themselves, as did Columbus, to be in the service of Jesus of Nazareth.

The people who are called black here, and who call themselves black, are a small and easily defeatable minority, somewhere around ten or twelve percent of us. They have nonetheless made what is perhaps this hemisphere's most consoling and harmlessly exciting contribution to world civilization: jazz. Second to that in making life a little better than it would be without it is, in my opinion, the therapeutic scheme for treating dangerous addictions, the invention by two white men in Akron, Ohio, of what are known as the Principles of Alcoholics Anonymous.

Two other men from Ohio invented the flying machine. But I don't believe we should be grateful to them. Such instruments have made smashing to smithereens the hopes of defenseless individuals, in Iraq, for example, even more of a lark than it was five hundred years ago.

* * *

And thus, with those lugubrious words, I end an idiosyncratic voyage of my own on paper. A kitchen chair set before a typewriter has been my caravel. A white tomcat has been my only crew. I have navigated by means of freely associated words and facts and people, starting with the number 1492. That reminded me somehow of my regimental commander years ago, and he reminded me somehow of the exploration of space, and on and on. I encountered raccoons and opossums on the way, and my first wife Jane, and Jesus and Hitler, and atomic submarines, and a virtuous young woman who was whipped until she behaved as though she had been brought up in a school for harlots, and Kirkpatrick Sale and Robert Hughes, and on and on.

The chance juxtaposing of Sale and Hughes gave me the only trinket worth saving, in my opinion, from the whole crazy trip, a definition of the grandeur Hughes and other good people find in history when viewed from a distance: the millions and millions of us who, in spite of all the atrocities, are still OK. The paying guests in evening clothes at a fund-raising banquet for the New York City Ballet Company in a ballroom at the Waldorf-Astoria Hotel come to mind. And how dare I speak ill of them, since I myself have been among them? I love the ballet.

* * *

I have just received a telephone call from a Canadian friend, a filmmaker who says that the planet can feed only six billion mammals our size, provided that the nourishment is fairly divided among us and delivered at once to anyone about to starve to death.

He has gathered together enough money to make a documentary film about the destruction by *Homo sapiens* of the planet, of "Space Ship Earth," as a life-support system. He asked me to be a consultant, since I had written, among other things, that we were "a new sort of glacier, warm-blooded and clever, unstoppable, about to gobble up everything and then make love—and then double in size again." He wants to wake us up.

***

His call interrupted my reading of this morning's mail, in which an old girlfriend from eons ago, now in the process of being divorced, sent me a newspaper clipping about a physician in Virginia, a specialist in the treatment of infertility in human beings. For years he had been giving women the benefit of sperm donated supposedly by strikingly healthy and intelligent and presentable young men. In at least eighty of the treatments that resulted in pregnancies carried to term, the donor had been the physician himself! So there is just one man who has added eighty more people to the burdens of the Earth. There aren't that many bears left in all of Germany, I heard on the radio this morning, nor elephants in Mozambique. And his kids are all going to want cars when they're old enough, and they'll reproduce.

A headwaiter in a hotel in Haiti, the scene of the only successful slave revolt in all of history, boasted to me that he had twenty-nine children. "I have very strong sperm," he said. And now corpses of whales are washing up on Long Island in industrial quantities. There could be a connection. Then again, the paint remover and the insecticides I put in my garbage cans last Tuesday could be to blame.

* * *

I am sorry not to be more encouraged and encouraging about human destiny in 1992, since I myself, with my reasonably strong sperm, have sired three children, and they have given me seven grandchildren in turn.

I am happy to say that all my descendants, mongrelized with Scottish and English and Irish genes, inhabit safe houses in peaceful neighborhoods, houses full of books and music and love and good things to eat. They are clearly beneficiaries of 1492 and all the rest of history when viewed from afar. But I can't see how that can go on much longer, since both hemispheres are now jam-packed with other people who need at least a thousand calories of nourishment every day. Indeed, starving men, women, and children are so numerous and ubiquitous now that our TV is hard put to show us even a minor fraction of them before making them disappear forever into the black hole in its wake.

As an anthropologist, supposedly, I might be expected to say a little something about the cultures that are vanishing along with the people. But hunger, it seems to me, becomes the whole of anybody's culture before death sets in. As Bertolt Brecht said, *"Erst kommt das Fressen, dann kommt die Moral,"* or, freely translated, "As long as we're hungry, all we can think about is food."

I agree with the Roman Catholic Church that all schemes for adjusting the human population to the food supply, short of abstinence exemplified by the last Tasmanians, range from indignity to infanticide. They are also impractical. My adopted son, the progeny of my late sister, served in the Peace Corps in a village on the eastern slope of the Andes in Peru. His mission was to discover what the little-known people there needed most, what a higher civilization might give to them. It turned out they wanted condoms, which are expensive, and which, of course, can be used only once and then must be thrown away. If he had been able to make condoms available, which our government surely would not have approved, they probably would have been tossed after use into a tributary of the Amazon River, coming to rest, at last, with any luck, on the beach at Ipanema, with all the nubile girls in their string bikinis.

So I have no choice but to say that the jig is up.

* * *

As consolation, I offer this prayer attributed to the great German-American theologian Reinhold Niebuhr (1892–1971), possibly as early as 1937, in the depths of the planetary economic depression before this one: "God grant me the serenity to accept the things I cannot change, courage to change the things I can, and wisdom to know the difference."

—Sagaponack, 1992

APPENDIX:
ROBOTVILLE AND MR. CASLOW

Editor's Note: The following is an unfinished science-fiction short story. While setting up a potentially fantastic tale, the story ends in mid-action, at the top of a typewritten manuscript page. It is not known whether an ending exists; to date, none has been found.

You return to your old public grade school on a gray day, just about sunset, when only the principal, the night janitor, and a child in trouble are there. You are passing through town by chance and return to your school on an impulse born of rootlessness. You have been away from the town for fifteen years, away from the planet itself for five. You have been on Mars. The grade school is one of the few places in the town of your childhood where someone may remember you still.

The concrete cornerstone of the school, roughed up to look like granite, says that the school is Number Fourteen: The Amos Crosby School. It takes you a moment to remember who Amos Crosby was. He was a whaling captain. The town was a whaling port once. Its nickname is still "The Harpoon City." It is mean and poor. Your father worked in a shoe factory here. The shoe factory closed. Your father and thousands more had had to move away.

You decipher the roman numeral on the cornerstone, calculate that the building was sixty-one years old at the start of World War III. The brutal pile of brick is seventy-six years old now. A big, bright new sign, shaped like an arrow, points away from the school, beguiling the eye with pictures of atoms and spaceships. "New Industrial Park," the sign reads; and, below that, "The Harpoon City Takes Its Rightful Place in the Age of Space." A vandal has been at work on the sign, writing big and scratching deep with something like a screwdriver. "Robotville," he has written in letters four feet high.

You already know about the New Industrial Park. The clerk at your hotel has told you about it. It is a vast tract of empty land, blessed by the mayor in a ribbon-cutting ceremony. It is supposed to tempt new industries into building there. So far, no new industries have built.

The wintry air lies still in the flat, thin light of sunset. It is not bitingly cold. Yet, what cold there is goes to the marrow of your bones. You gradually understand that it is a sense of desolation that makes you cold. Nine out of every ten houses along the street are dark, empty, for sale.

You wonder if your old school is still a school. You see that it is, for there are long bicycle racks on the playground. There is a single bicycle in the racks, the bicycle, surely, of the boy kept long after school. It is the bare skeleton of a bicycle, without fenders or chainguard or handlebar grips. The skeleton is rusty.

You go to the front doors, find them locked by the same crude method used in your own day. A padlocked chain is strung through the brass handles inside. You shake the door, rattling the chain. You remember this as the customary way for calling the night janitor.

You already know that the janitor won't be Mr. Pensington, the janitor in your day. You know that Mr. Pensington died in the war, in the Home Guard stand against the robots at Louisville. You remember him fondly as a giant who had majestic contempt for any child who did not please his teacher.

Now a new janitor comes up the iron treads from the basement. You feel an unfair dislike—disliking him for not being Mr. Pensington. He is in his thirties; lean, hawk-faced, balding some. He comes up the stairs eagerly, expecting someone else. He shows disappointment when he sees you, doesn't want to let you in.

"You from the committee?" he calls through the glass. He lets you know with the tone of his voice that he doesn't want to be bothered by anybody who isn't on the committee.

"No," you say. You try to impress him with a name that, for all you know, may be meaningless to him. "I want to see Mr. Caslow," you say. Caslow was the school principal in your day. The probability of his still being principal is low.

This makes the janitor furtive, suspicious. "You on *his* side?" he says. Obviously, Caslow is on one side of a dispute, and the janitor is on the other.

"I used to go here," you say.

"You come back some other time," he says. "Caslow can't see you now. He's waiting for the committee." He starts to walk away.

You are furious. "Hey!" you shout at his back, and you make the door chain rattle. He stops, looks at you uneasily. You think he must be a moron. It isn't his face that tells you so. It is the fact that he is wearing proudly what you have not seen in years—a discharge button from World War III. Not even in the first months following the war did anyone but a fool wear his discharge button. It was no distinction to have served in the armed forces—not in a war in which the old men and the women and even the children had turned out to fight robots. Yet, years after the war, here is a queer duck who seems to think his discharge button is a great badge of honor.

You yell a big lie at him. "Better let me in!" you say. "I'm a friend of the mayor!" The hotel clerk has told you that the mayor is a hustler, a comer—but you've forgotten the mayor's name.

Your yell hits the janitor harder than you expect. He is afraid to believe you, afraid not to. He touches the crown of his head as though there is something magic up there that will tell him what to do. The gesture is a dead giveaway. It is the gesture of an ex-prisoner of war. The janitor is touching the fine, silver-wire antenna that enemy surgeons put under his scalp. The antenna used to tell him exactly what to do. The antenna used to take radio signals out of the air, send them into his brain. The antenna, during the war, was what made him be a robot.

* * *

You do not hate him for having been a robot. He could not help himself. His life from the time the wire was installed until the war ended was a blank. He simply woke up one day to be told that the war was over, that he was free. No one was going to radio-control him anymore. While radio-controlled, he had done prodigies of work and killing for the enemy. He could not be blamed.

If the sight of him makes you slightly queasy, it is out of pity for him. The few ex-robots you have known have hated themselves for what they did in the war. Worse than that, they have had to live with the knowledge that they might at any moment be turned into robots again. Tampering with the apparatus the enemy put in their minds would result in certain death.

Laws protect them. It is a crime of the most serious sort to send out radio signals in the range of frequencies known as "the robot band." That band is not to be used until the last ex-robot is dead.

Now the ex-robot school janitor decides reluctantly to let you in. He unlocks the chain, opens the door. "You really a friend of Mayor Jack's?" he says.

"Mayor Jack and I are like that," you say, and you waggle crossed fingers under his nose.

You step inside, are filled with nostalgia by the faint school smell. It has not changed. You wonder what its ingredients are. Chalk, soft coal, and children's breaths? You remember what a glorious old fortress of freedom the ramshackle school really was—is. The place is still vibrant with brave, lovely, childish contempt for anyone who would not be free.

"The mayor's late," says the janitor.

"He's been held up," you say with a knowing smile.

"The mayor's gotta come," says the janitor, "or the old man will just tie up the committee in knots again."

"Old man?" you say.

"Caslow," says the janitor, surprised that you should ask. "Who else?" His hand goes to the crown of his head again. "The mayor *is* gonna fire him tonight, isn't he?" he says. "They really got the goods on him this time."

You nod, become worried and watchful. Something sinister is going on.

The janitor comes closer, so you can hear him whisper. "I know who's been tearing down the posters," he says. He shakes his head. "It isn't the kids. It's the old man himself!" He goes to a trash barrel by a bulletin board, pulls out two rumpled posters. "I saw him tear these down with his own hands an hour ago."

You examine the posters. "Ex-prisoners of war are human, too—" says one, "respect their special needs." The quotation is credited to Mayor Harlan Jack. The accompanying picture shows an idealized family that appears to be seeing God. They are looking, however, at nothing more supernatural than a radio mast. The other poster shows a tragically handsome man. The fingers of his right hand rest lightly on the crown of his head. Like the janitor, he wears his discharge button proudly. "He only asks to serve to the very *fullest*," reads the poster. Mayor Jack is supposed to have said that, too. And both posters, you see, have been published by something called the Committee of Friends of Ex-Prisoners of War.

Your feeling of nightmare increases. It makes no sense that the ex-prisoners of war would have such active, passionate friends. To the best of your knowledge, they have never been discriminated against, have never been treated in any way that would make them feel in a class apart. The few thousand that survived the war dispersed very quickly, became ordinary citizens with ordinary ups and downs. You can't imagine why they should gather, why they should draw attention to themselves as a group.

You grope for more clues. "I—I see you're wearing your discharge button," you say.

"Mayor Jack said to, didn't he?" says the janitor anxiously. "Did he say, 'Take 'em off now'?" His hand goes to the button, ready to yank it off at the mayor's command.

"No, no—" you say, "you keep right on wearing it till the mayor tells you different." You overplay your hand, thinking mistakenly that Mayor Jack is staging a general patriotic revival. "Dressed in such a hurry this morning," you say, "I forgot to put my button on."

He claps you on the arm, loves you like a brother. "You're an ex-POW, too!" he says.

You nod. It isn't true.

"How come I never see you at the meetings?" he says.

"I've been out of town," you say.

"Have you signed the petition—the latest one?" he says. Plainly, your answer is important to him.

"Not yet," you say at last.

He pulls a petition from his overalls' pocket, forces you to take it and a pen. "Sign," he says.

You read the petition. "We, the undersigned ex-prisoners of war," you read, "respectfully urge the immediate passage of Public Bill 1126, the Morris-Ames-McLellan Bill, permitting the use of robot labor in industry." The janitor's petition, a very dim carbon copy, has perhaps thirty signatures on it.

Your disgust is so profound that you simply let the pen and petition fall to the floor. You walk away, mount the stairs to the first-floor hallway, go down the hallway to Mr. Caslow's office. You understand now that the ex-prisoners of war, the ex-robots, are begging to be used as robots again.

***

You come quietly to Mr. Caslow's office door. His office is unchanged from your day. There is the same public-building shabbiness—battered furniture, exposed pipes, chipped paint that lets dirty beiges and greens show through from years gone by. And there are the same old relics of freedom and nature and civilization—a framed replica of the Declaration of Independence, a plaster bust of Shakespeare, a portrait of George Washington, an oriole's nest, gay curtains made by the home economics class... The Third World War, you note with pleasure, has not necessitated the addition or subtraction of a single relic.

A ten-year-old boy, owner of the lonely bicycle outside, sits in a wooden armchair. He is unused to arms on chairs, runs his moist palms up and down them, seeking a resting place, finding none.

Mr. Caslow sits at his desk, paying no attention to the restless boy. Mr. Caslow is gravely signing certificates of some sort. He does not seem worried about the coming of the mayor and the committee. You clear your throat loudly, and he is not startled, does not look up at once. You remember him as a game, stocky, decent man in his forties, as poor as Job's turkey. He is remarkably unchanged physically, save for his hair. His hair is white now.

"Yes?" he says, looking up at last. "Are you the advance party?"

You smile. "Of what, sir?" you say.

"Of the committee—of the bleeding hearts society," he says.

"No, sir," you say. "I used to go to school here. I just wanted to look in and say hello." You tell him your name.

He seems amazed. He blinks several times, then stands, welcomes you in. "You'll excuse me if I seem a little rusty at welcoming a student back," he says. "Not many come back these days." He turns to the boy. "Aaron," he says, "go down in the basement and see if you can't help your father. When the committee comes, you and your father come up with them."

"Yes, sir," says Aaron respectfully. He leaves.

Mr. Caslow waits until Aaron is out of earshot, and then he says to you, "Not many graduates come back since they took over the neighborhood."

"Who?" you say.

"The ex-prisoners of war," he says. "That's all we've got here now, you know—children of the robots. One hundred percent."

"Are—are they any different from other children?" you say.

"No," says Caslow. He gives a bitter grin. "Unfortunately for their parents—no." He looks at his watch. "That's what the committee is coming to see me about tonight. They're late. I should know by now that it's a mathematical impossibility for a committee to do anything on time."

You ask Mr. Caslow about the seeming series of unrelated mysteries—the committee, the petition, the posters, the gathering of the ex-prisoners of war, the boy in trouble, the Industrial Park, the wearing of the dis-charge buttons—and he tells you that they are all one.

In explaining this unity, the good old man gets only as far as the case of the boy, of Aaron the janitor's son. "It was Aaron," he says, "who defaced the new sign outside, wrote Robotville on it." He smiles ruefully. "It is an eight-hundred-dollar sign," he says, "erected at public expense. And now a child with strong wrists and a fifteen-cent screwdriver has made the sign say exactly what the mayor and the committee can't stand to have said."

And then the mayor and the committee arrive.

* * *

The chain rattles at the front doors below. The janitor exclaims greetings as he unlocks the chain. He is a new man, garrulous and merry, now that his friends are here. When the doors open, School Number Fourteen is filled with self-important grumbling, and with the barking sounds committee members make as they congratulate each other on every step they take.

Someone in the entourage thinks there ought to be more of a reception. "His Honor the mayor's here!" he shouts.

"Now, Stan," says a liquid tenor voice that surely belongs to the mayor, "let's not come in here acting like the mayor is the queen of France."

"Is *this* the boy?" says a woman's voice. She is ready to cry, if the answer is yes.

The woman does cry—or makes crying sounds. You guess that she is embarrassing the boy with hugs now. "You didn't know what you were writing on that sign, did you?" she says. She answers for him. "Of course you didn't!"

Other voices agree that the boy couldn't possibly be so wicked as to know the full, awful meaning of what he wrote.

Now the group mounts the stairs, approaches Caslow's office.

Caslow sits at his desk again, so as to be found as you found him—gravely signing certificates. He realizes that you are in an odd position. He wants you to stay. "You can pretend to be my lawyer," he says, and he means it. "That will absolutely stupefy them—set them back six months." He chuckles. "Imagine a grade-school principal insisting on legal rights, just as though he were a parent!"

You are flattered. And the ham actor in you makes you think that you may give a surprisingly good performance as a lawyer.

The mayor appears in the doorway, heading the procession. He has young Aaron by the hand. The mayor is himself boyish—and pink and porky and beautifully dressed. He has the radiant look peculiar to bullies. That is, Mayor Jack assumes that he is lovable because so many people go to so much trouble to keep on the right side of him.

He startles you by studying you for a moment, then calling you by name. You really do know him. You were classmates at School Number Fourteen. His Honor, Mayor Harlan Jack, is the man a boy named Happy Jack became. The boy named Happy Jack, you remember, had a stunning talent for putting noble interpretations on his endless acts of greed. You note that Mayor Jack the man is now massaging young Aaron's neck, doing his best to dull the boy's lively mind.

"My lawyer," Mr. Caslow says of you.

He is correct in his prediction. The committee shows dismay at his having legal counsel.

"Now he has a lawyer!" says the woman who cried over Aaron. She says it as though Mr. Caslow had pulled a gun. You catch a glimpse of her over Mayor Jack's shoulder. She looks like a turtle, with the addition of steel-rimmed spectacles and a bristly tweed coat.

Now the head of a black minister bobs into view, tragic with the sufferings of a minority that no longer suffers as a minority. "This isn't any question for lawyers," he says. "This is a question for God."

"That's right!" says Mayor Jack hotly. He marches on short, thick legs to Caslow's desk, separates you from your supposed client, glares at you. "We're not here to fuss around with legal technicalities," he says. "We're not here to weep and wail about an eight-hundred-dollar sign being ruined, either! We're here to talk about what that sign business is a symptom of! In the area surrounding School Number Fourteen, parental authority has broken down completely. And we're here to do what we can," says Mayor Jack fervently, "to pull those families back together again."

Mayor Jack orders the local chapter of the Committee of Friends of Ex-Prisoners of War to come in. And in they come, the people Mr. Caslow has called "the bleeding hearts society." You fight an impulse to laugh. The people, taken together, are a wild satire on all bleeding hearts societies from the beginning of time. You ransack your mind for an apt description—think of *living statues* and discard it. The solemn folk haven't the roundness of statues. And then you get it right—they are comporting themselves as a living letterhead. Every decent element in town is represented, so graphically represented that the group seems to be almost a costume drama.

After appreciating their flamboyant differences, you look for things the members have in common. You find three such things: at least moderate prosperity, eagerness to be led by the noblest emotions, and an undiscriminating pity for underdogs, a pity that is plainly as big as all outdoors.

Above all, their hearts are in the right place.

Ten of them crowd into the office, followed by a cigar-chewing aide to the mayor, the janitor, and finally a man who does not belong in such company, or even in such a town. He is sleek, elegant, superior, and shrewd. His nostrils indicate that the school smells bad. His presence makes the mayor look like a bumpkin, an oaf.

Mr. Caslow immediately singles the man out as the only person worth talking to. "I don't believe I've seen that gentleman back there before," says Caslow.

"Merely an observer," says the man, and makes himself small.

"Will you introduce us?" Caslow says to the mayor.

"I'm not at liberty to tell you the gentleman's name at present," says the mayor. He likes the sound of these words, thinks he has handled the situation with grace.

The man thinks the mayor has handled the situation stupidly. "Ansel B. Rybolt is my name," he says curtly. "No secret."

"Are you an educator, Mr. Rybolt?" says Caslow. "Is that why you came to observe?"

Mayor Jack, attempting to regain the floor, now blunders in the opposite direction, tells too much about the man. "He's a manufacturer," he says, "and I may say he's thinking very hard about putting up a sizeable plant in the Industrial Park."

Caslow claps his hands. "Aha!" he says. "Now everything is crystal clear!" He nods to you. "Now we know exactly what it is Mr. Rybolt has come to observe."

Rybolt is so fed up with the mayor's blundering that he attempts to stalk out. But he finds the doorway blocked by the janitor.

"You really thinking of building here?" says the janitor.

"I've made no commitments whatsoever," says Rybolt, wanting to get by.

"You wouldn't be sorry!" says the janitor. His voice is harsh because he is wishing so hard for the new plant. "I'd work like *hell* for you!" he says. And he launches himself into an almost delirious account of the prodigies of work he accomplished during the war as a robot.

Ansel B. Rybolt rolls his eyes, begging the mayor or someone to get the creature away from him.

"I'm no good to anybody the way I am," says the janitor to Rybolt. "But you radio-control me, and I'll do the work of ten good men and charge the price of one!"

"Now isn't the time to discuss that," says Mayor Jack. "Just shut up about that for now."

The janitor subsides. Rybolt

ABOUT THE AUTHOR

Kurt Vonnegut (1922–2007) is one of the most beloved American writers of the twentieth century. Vonnegut began his career as a science fiction writer, and his early novels—*Player Piano* and *The Sirens of Titan*—were categorized as such even as they appealed to an audience far beyond the reach of the category. In the 1960s, Vonnegut became closely associated with the baby boomer generation, a writer on that side, so to speak. Scholars believe that Vonnegut's reputation (like Mark Twain's) will grow steadily through the decades as his work continues to increase in relevance and new connections are formed, new insights made.

Kindle *Serials*

This book was originally released in episodes as a Kindle Serial. Kindle Serials launched in 2012 as a new way to experience serialized books. Kindle Serials allow readers to enjoy the story as the author creates it, purchasing once and receiving all existing episodes immediately, followed by future episodes as they are published. To find out more about Kindle Serials and to see the current selection of Serials titles, visit www.amazon.com/kindleserials.